The

Somnambulist's

Dreams

2016 Angry Owl Publishing © All rights reserved

Copyright © Lars Boye Jerlach

Printed in the United States of America

Cover design and artwork by Kyle Louis Fletcher www.usklf.com

ISBN-13: 978-0692746608 (Angry Owl Publishing)

ISBN-10: 0692746609

The

Somnambulist's Dreams

A novel by

Lars Boye Jerlach

To Tom,

[signature]

I hope you'll enjoy....

 ANGRY OWL

For Helen, Amelia, Omi and Louisa

There was no denying it was lonesome.

Now that the frost had irrevocably moved down from the north, he found the nights particularly long. He rubbed his hands over the kerosene stove in the galley, before putting on his fingerless gloves and wrapping a thick grey woolen scarf around his neck. His uniform was far from adequate, so to keep warm he picked up his overcoat, put two of the heated stones in his coat pockets and climbed the stairs. It was cold in the watch room, and as he exhaled, small shapeless clouds formed in the air.

He put down the lamp on a small battered rectangular oak table on which a number of initials and other inscriptions had been veraciously carved, removed a watch from his pocket and flipped open the cover to check the time.

Not that it was necessary.

The sun was still dispersing a sheath of liquid fire on the horizon, so he still had some time.

As usual he had cleaned and inspected the lens earlier that morning. He had also refilled the fuel and checked the wick. Although it was somewhat frayed, he hadn't found it necessary to trim it.

He began winding up the mechanism that rotated the Fresnel

lens. He counted the revolutions and when he could feel the proper resistance from the weights, he stopped and looked out at the sky that, with its millions of effulgent flecks, stretched above him in an infinite elastic expanse. At least tonight he wouldn't have to worry about visibility.

After he had lit the wick and set the lens in motion, the light would be flashing for the next hour and a half, before it needed another rewind.

He stared into the night and listened to the wind lambaste the waves against the granite, almost sixty feet below. He could almost sense their febrile, liquid tentacles surrounding the belfry as the tide moved in.

He was fascinated by the facility and seemingly infinite power of the ocean, and in his first few months in the tower he had often devoted his entire watch to gazing at the sea, utterly lost in the immensity before him.

He unbuttoned the top of his coat to remove a small package that he set down on the table next to the lamp. He repositioned one of the rickety armless chairs and sat down.

He had found the package earlier in the day, when he had cleared out the small storage area next to the water cistern on the lower level. Something light had been hastily wrapped in an old waxy piece of paper and tied together with a piece of oily twine.

Due to its lack of substance he had almost discarded it, but then he read the faded fragment: *".....ust acquaint themselves with the working of the apparatus in their charge. Upon any doubtful point questions must be a ...."* on the outside of the pallid but dirty paper.

He recognized it from the booklet, *Instructions to Lighthouse-Keepers by authority of The Lighthouse Board.* Before taking up his current position he had read it studiously, and he had even brought his own copy of the 1881 edition with him. It was now sitting in the small bookshelf by the bed, in the sleeping quarters on the second floor.

He had put the small package aside and after he had finished clearing out and rearranging the storage area, he carried it upstairs and put it on the small stool next to his bed. Although he was intrigued by its content, he nevertheless decided to wait until evening to properly examine it.

He had left it on the stool as he slept.

Now it was time.

He put his hands in his pockets and closed his fingers around the warm smooth unyielding surface of the heated stones.

He realized that he would have most likely appeared deranged to the casual observer, as he had walked up and down the beach picking up, examining, comparing and rejecting a great number of stones until he found four that were as close to faultless as they could be.

The surfaces of the specimens he had finally selected were completely smooth and when he closed his fingers around them, they fitted comfortably in the palm of his hands. They were all slightly irregular in shape and placed together on the stove in the galley, they very much looked like a small pile of grey tapered potatoes. He rolled the stones around in his pockets until his fingertips started to prickle.

When his fingers had regained their mobility, he picked up the small parcel, untied the twine and unfolded the paper to expose a small bundle of papers.

He twice folded the waxy cover paper, pressed it down with his hand, and placed the rolled up twine on top. He put it at the corner of the table and looked at the bundle in front of him.

The papers were small, not much bigger than a regular postcard, and nearly translucent.

When he carefully removed the top piece from the pile and held it up to the light, he felt like he was holding something evanescent between his fingertips.

The paper flowed against his skin like a thin membrane and the words decorated the page in a fluid, intricate pattern.

He thought of the wings of a butterfly as he gingerly placed it on the table and read.

The Dreams of

Enoch S. Soule

My Dearest Emily,

When we were young, you often asked me what I dreamed about in the night and though I was always reluctant to tell you, mostly because I was embarrassed and fearful of your response, I have finally decided to write to you about my dreams, and trust that you will recognize and know the true me and not be abhorred by the fantasies of my mind, over which I have no control.

I am, as far as I know, compos mentis and yet I cannot explain, even to myself, where the figments originate. Beside their esotericism, I do not know if there is any other significance to them.

I have chosen to share my dreams with you, so that you can better understand and perhaps accept why I could not share them sooner.

The dreams have always been the same, and despite some slight variations, they have not changed for as long as I can remember. I have attempted to name the places that I visit, though without proper research, I cannot be sure if they hold true. I have not ordered or dated the dreams, as it seems that there is no beginning or end to them. They flow into one another, like a stroke from a painter's brush, to form one complete but enigmatic picture.

However, before I tell you what transpires in my somnambular state, I want you to know, how truly sorry I am to have left you lonely all these years. It was never my intent for us to be apart for such an extensive amount of time. I hope you can find it in your heart to forgive me.

Although you have said in jest many times, that I was in love only with my tower, you should know that, from the depths of my heart, there has never been anyone else on this earth that I loved more than you.

Blessed Mary herself has but a morsel of the affection of my heart as you do. You have always been and will always be my one true love and our beautiful girls my eternal inspiration.

Sitting here overlooking the expanse of the sea, I wish that I could rewind time, so that I could have devoted more of it to being at home with you and the girls, instead of being locked away in this tower, listening to the eternal thrashing of the waves.

Alas, that is not possible.

In the end we all must accept and live the life we have chosen with the happiness and misgivings that follow.

You have never complained or lamented your lot in life, however, I am deeply sorry if I have brought you more heartache than joy, both in our time together and apart.

I would like you to know, that I believe my time here is coming to an end. These days my body is in near constant agony and my mind has started to wander, even more so than usual.

I miss the sight of the trees in the street, the smell of flowers in the garden,

the sound of small songbirds and the laughter of our girls. But mostly I miss

having my arms around You in a loving embrace.

I bide my time until we meet.

Please pass on my everlasting love and affection to the girls.

I will forever be yours.

Your Loving Husband,

Enoch

He turned over the page; it was blank. He looked through the window into the darkness and searched the horizon. Nothing was moving but the sea.

He wondered how the package had found its way to the tool cupboard in the storage area.

When he looked down he realized he was still holding the letter between his fingers.

He carefully placed it face down on the table next to the bundle and picked up the next sheet.

Kenya

I was standing under an unusual tree that, as far as I could tell was the only source of shade for miles around.

The air was tremendously warm and very dry.

I was hot, but not uncomfortably so, as I was wearing very little clothing.

My body was completely bare, but for a kind of loincloth tied around my waist and a vivid red blanket slung over my shoulder.

I could feel a heavy necklace of beads around my neck and I was holding a spear in my right hand.

As I looked at it, I noticed that my skin was dark and that my fingers were extremely long.

I opened and closed my left hand, stomped my naked feet on the ground, and created a small cloud of dust that quickly dissipated.

Apart from some erratically distributed brushy vegetation and the giant tree under which I stood, the surrounding area looked completely barren. I could hear the familiar call of a crow or a raven in the crown above me, but even as I shaded my eyes with my hand to search the treetop, I couldn't see it. As I lowered my hand a small white bracelet slid down my wrist. It seemed the beads were made of some kind of bone.

I looked into the horizon.

The heat made the entire landscape seem like a mirage and I found it difficult to see if anything moved in the distance.

Beside me on the ground lay a strange looking creature. It mostly resembled a bull, yet not a breed with which I was familiar. It was a whitish sandy colour with a peculiar hump above its shoulders. Its curvy horns were sticking up about a hand's length from its long, narrow head and its ears, pointing downwards, were swatting at the flies crawling around its head. It swung its head from side to side and looked up at me.

"Who are you?" it said.

I jumped in surprise, and quickly looked around to see where the voice was coming from. There was nobody else around. I thought that the conditions might be playing tricks with my mind.

I looked at the bull on the ground.

"Who are you, and why are you here?" it asked. The voice was as clear in my head, as if the bull had actually spoken.

I continued to look at it in disbelief. "You are no longer Sironka," it said, "so you must be someone else. Who are you?"

"I am Enoch Soule," I said, when I had gotten over my initial shock. Actually, I wasn't sure if I had spoken the words aloud.

"What are you doing here?" the bull asked again.

"I don't know," I said, looking around, "where are we?"

"We are here," The bull said, licking its muzzle.

"Where is here?" I asked.

"This is here," the bull replied, shaking its ears to repel the flies.

"That doesn't really answer my question."

"In what way does that not that answer your question?"

The bull looked at me.

"Because I am not any closer to making sense of where I am." I looked around. "Does this place have a name?"

"The name of the place is here," the bull said, "and here is where we are."

"That's ridiculous," I said, "this place must have a name, otherwise how would you know the difference between here and there." I pointed in direction of the horizon.

"That is simple," the bull replied, "when you are in motion, everything changes. There is always where here is not."

"That doesn't make sense," I said, "that's just saying that we are always here."

"That's what I just said," the bull replied, without a hint of irony.

"So what are you doing here?" I asked.

"Lying on the ground, talking to you," it answered.

"That much is obvious" I said, more than a little annoyed, "but how did you get here?"

"I followed Sironka, who led me here," it answered.

"Do you know why he led you here?" I asked.

"Yes," the bull replied, "here is the place I cease to exist".

"Why?" I asked.

"Because it is time," it replied.

"How do you know?"

"There is no knowing, only culmination," the bull said swinging its tail.

I didn't reply. Instead I looked into the distance.

"What do you think you are you doing here?" it asked.

"I haven't got the faintest idea," I replied. "It is a mystery to me. I am the keeper of a lighthouse."

"What is a lighthouse?" the bull asked.

"It's a tall tower that is built in or near the ocean by the coast." I answered. "It is normally white and lit up in the night to warn the ships that land is near."

"What is the ocean?" it asked.

"It's a tremendously huge amount of water, that covers most of the surface of the earth," I answered.

"What is the earth?"

"The earth is where we are."

"It can't be," the bull replied, "you said that the ocean covers most of the surface of the earth, yet here it is completely dry."

"Earth is an enormous place, with many different variants. Just because it is dry here, doesn't mean it is dry everywhere else. Did you not say that everything changes when we are in motion? I have traveled far and experienced many changes, yet I have never encountered what you describe. The place that you call earth must therefore be very different from here." The bull looked at me and cocked its head.

"Although it is different from here, it still belongs to the same entity," I said. "Everything around us is just smaller fragments of a much, much larger whole."

"It cannot be different from here and part of here at the same time." The bull looked at me. "Everything cannot be the same."

"I didn't say they were the same, I said they were small fragments of a larger whole," I said somewhat exasperated.

"But if the ocean is tremendously huge, it cannot possibly be a small fragment." The bull dragged its front legs underneath its body.

"It's difficult to explain," I said, scratching my head, that I then realized was clean shaven. "The earth is an immense and very complicated place that consists of a great number of elements that in combination make our lives here possible."

I looked at the bull to see if he understood.

"It is good for us that we are here then," it said shaking its head.

I heard the sound of an engine in the distance and turned around to see where the sound was coming from. I spotted a cloud of dust moving towards us and before long a moss coloured automobile with an open top, pulled up and skidded to a halt about twenty feet away from the tree.

The driver turned off the engine, jumped down from the vehicle and walked over to where I was standing. Although my time with the bull had been sufficiently surprising, I was nevertheless taken aback by the fact that the driver was a fairly young woman. She was probably in her late twenties to early thirties. Her face was elongated with sharply defined features. She had a somewhat pointy chin and high cheekbones and her dark, deep-set eyes were bright and alert. Her long brown hair was tied back and covered under a large-brimmed hat. She was wearing a slightly oversized sand coloured safari outfit that looked like it had been fashioned at the beginning of the century. She had rolled up the sleeves on her shirt exposing her slender but strong arms. A small white kerchief was loosely tied around her neck and her long shorts were held up by a heavy leather belt.

A pair of brown dusty leather boots completed her outfit.

She strode up to me.

"Good day to you Sironka," she said, "I saw you from the car. What are you doing out here?" She looked at me searchingly.

I did not know what to say or what to do, so I looked at the bull instead. It looked back at me.

"She is a friend of Sironka's," it said. "Tell her why you are here."

"But I don't know why I'm here." I said, realizing that the woman was waiting for my answer and apparently couldn't hear the conversation between the bull and myself.

"Tell her instead why Sironka is here," the bull said.

I turned to face the woman.

"I am here because my bull is dying." I gestured towards the bull, that now turned its head and looked at the woman.

"Oh, I am truly sorry to hear that." She walked over and crouched down next to the bull and began to swat at the flies with her hand.

"I know how much he means to you." She stroked the front of the bull's head.

"Yes" I said, looking at the bull, "he is very important to me."

"Do you mind if I stay a while? I really don't want to intrude, but I would really appreciate it." She looked up at me, and when I didn't object, she sat down next to the bull.

"What's his name?" she asked. "I know you have already told me, but I am afraid I have forgotten."

I ransacked my mind for a name that would suit the bull, but the only name I could think of was Otis. "Please tell me your name," I asked the bull, which appeared to be oblivious to my plea. "Please tell me."

"Kongoni is what you called me," it answered.

"His name is Kongoni," I said to the woman who was now sitting cross-legged next to the bull.

"Oh yes, I remember. It's the Maasai name for what we call the Hartebeest," she said. "You can clearly see the resemblance." She ran her *hand along the length of the bull's head.*

"What happens when he passes away?" She looked at the bull.

"He ceases to exist here," I answered.

"That is a beautiful sentiment Sironka," she said looking up at me. "Does that mean that he will continue to exist somewhere else?"

"I hope so," I said.

"Do you continue your existence somewhere else?" I asked Kongoni the bull.

"I hope so," it said.

"I realize it is probably the most inopportune time to tell you this," the woman said, still stroking the front of the bulls' head, "but I want you to know that I love your country with all my soul, Sironka. I can honestly say that I haven't been happier anywhere else in the world and I wish I could stay here forever."

When she looked at me, there were tears in her eyes.

"Tell her that she will be here forever," Kongoni said.

"You will be here forever," I told her.

"I really hope so," she said, "but I am not so sure that is possible. Forever is a very long time." She got to her feet and brushed the dust off her shorts.

"I'd better be going," she said. "Thank you so much for letting me stay with Kongoni for a while. It means a great deal to me."

She bent down, put her hand on the bull's head and whispered: "My hope is, that when you cease to exist here, you will continue your existence elsewhere." With her hand still fixed on the head of the bull, everything around us seemed to lose definition.

It was as if every single particle in the world began to simultaneously drift apart, dissolving in an ocean of tiny multi-coloured specks.

"I am ceasing to exist here," said the bull.

I awoke standing by the window in the watch room, overlooking the sea. The sun was high in the sky and the room was as hot as a furnace. I was wearing nothing but my underwear and holding the shaft of an old broom in my hand.

Although I am intrigued by my chimeras and accept that they are somehow connected, I will not attempt to analyze this or any of my other dreams, but leave them for you or others to interpret.

All I can do, is give you a faithful description of what transpires in my somnambular state.

He put down the page and got up from his chair.

The stones were getting cold in his pockets.

He pulled out his watch and checked the time. In twenty minutes he would have to rewind the mechanism.

He walked down the stairs to the galley, where he placed his lamp and the cold stones on the end of the stove. He grabbed the small black kettle and gently shook it, listening to the water splashing about within.

He placed it on the small yet heavy iron cast stove and retrieved the blue and white china teapot from the lime green cupboard. The teapot was much used and the spout was a bit cracked. Painted in a watery blue glaze on its orbicular belly, two small swallows were swooping over a diminutive fruit tree. He placed the pot at the end of the stove and checked the supply of tea on the top shelf, before measuring out enough leaves to make a brew that wasn't too weak.

He checked his watch again. Twelve minutes.

He waited for the water to boil.

He knew it wouldn't take long.

While he waited, he poured a bit of hot water into the teapot and swished it around, looking at the rising steam. He then poured the still warm water into his cup.

When he had first arrived in the tower, the cup had been as white as a piano key. Overcome by constant immersion, the inside was now the colour of amber, and no matter how hard he'd scrubbed at it, he hadn't been able to stop the fine dark crackling web that was slowly emerging on its surface.

He poured the boiling water over the leaves and looked as they swirled in the hot stream, like a shoal of small fish. He replaced the lid and poured the tepid water from his cup back into the kettle.

He checked the time. Six minutes.

He put the two hot stones in his pockets, picked up the teapot and cup with one hand, and the lamp with the other. He made his way back upstairs.

As he maneuvered the teapot and the mug onto the table, he was careful not to spill.

He walked over to rewind the mechanism.

He looked out over the ocean.

Only a small flock of white seagulls, bobbing up and down on the surface near the rocks, interrupted the monotony of the sea. He sat down at the table and removed his gloves. He cupped his cold calloused hands, blew into them and rubbed them together. He then put the gloves back on and lifted the teapot off the table and gently swirled the tea around. He waited for the leaves to settle before pouring a small amount of tea into his cup. It was still lacking in colour, so he put the pot back on the table.

In the absence of a tea cozy, he removed his scarf and wrapped it around the pot.

He flipped up the collar of his black coat, buttoned the top button and pulled the collar tight around his neck.

He thought of the lighthouse keeper's dream.

Besides the dioramas at the Museum of Natural History, his knowledge of Africa was minimal.

He didn't recognize the bull from the description in the dream and wondered if it was another figment of Soule's imagination, or whether such a creature actually existed.

He was also curious about the identity of the woman. It somehow seemed unlikely that a young white woman would be out in the African bush by herself.

He wondered what was she doing in Kenya and how she had known the Maasai.

Although he accepted the dream as a complete fantasy, there was however something distinctive in the description of the landscape and the conversation between the bull and the Maasai.

He couldn't quite shake the feeling that Enoch Soule had believed it all to be real.

He filled his cup with the steaming amber coloured liquid and touched it to his hardened, chapped lips, before returning the cup to the table.

He checked his watch.

An hour and fifteen minutes.

He picked up a new sheet from the bundle.

The Antarctic

I fell on the ice.

When I tried to stand up, I couldn't feel my hands nor my feet. I was wearing a fur lined hat, pulled down to cover my ears, and the lower part of my face was wrapped in a thick woolen scarf. A pair of giant sealskin gloves, tied to my coat with a peculiar harness, covered my hands. A pair of fur boots enveloped my feet and the lower part of my legs.

I was in a rough and furfuraceous landscape, as I imagined the surface of an alien planet might be, consumed by a ferocious wind that bit into my face with tiny needle sharp teeth. Besides four barely visible objects in the distance, all I could see was snow and ice. I was standing still, while the elements around me continued their howling onslaught.

I tried to move, but my limbs negated my command.

I heard somebody shouting in the distance.

"Oates? Oates?"

The voice was coming closer, until a weather-beaten face appeared out of the storm. It was difficult to say how old this man was. His face was red and blistered from the exposure. He had small icicles hanging from his eyebrows and the lower part of his face was, as my own, covered in a heavy scarf. His eyes were looking at me from behind a large pair of goggles and he was otherwise dressed exactly as me.

"You have to move Soldier," he said, "you have to move."

"I am trying," I said "but It seems I have no more fuel left in the tank."

"Nonsense," he shouted. "You need to get moving. It's imperative we get to the depot."

"Alright," I said, "I'll do my best."

"That's all I ask," he said, and grabbed my arm to pull me along.

Although I could see he had taken hold of me, I couldn't feel it.

I tried to move with him, but there was nothing I could do, my legs were inert.

I fell down on the ice and scraped my cheek against the glacial surface, but I didn't feel any pain.

"Oates you have to get up," he shouted, "you have to get up, right now!"

I tried to stand, but my entire body now felt immobile.

"Wilson," he shouted, over the howling wind, "Bowers, hold up. Hold up."

"Hang in there, Soldier," he said, "I'll be back soon."

He slapped me on my shoulder and left me on the ice.

There was nothing but the violent cold and the turbulent wind to keep me company. I closed my eyes.

I believed I could hear voices in the distance. At first I thought it was an illusion, brought on by the elements, but the voices grew in strength.

"Oates," they shouted, in discord, "Oates, where are you?" "Here." I shouted back. My voice sounded weak and exhausted.

"Here. I am over here."

I feebly tried to raise my arm to wave, but it felt as heavy as lead and all I managed to do was to roll it slightly away from my body; even that small action was painful.

I wasn't sure that anybody had heard me, but soon three faces were looking down at me.

"This is no time for a nap, old boy," one of them said, as they grabbed me under my arms and slowly got me up to a standing position.

"I am sorry," I said "but I can't go on." I hung on their shoulders, as my legs again gave out from under me.

"He needs to rest, Robert," said one of the men. "We all need to rest."

"I know, Birdie," he replied. I could tell he was weighing his options.

"Let us set up camp and pray for a turn in the weather," he said.

They lowered me to the ground.

I was pretty much useless and could only watch as they unpacked the sledge and began raising the tent. It was an arduous task and it took them a long time to finish.

Once the tent was up, they helped me inside and lowered me onto a bunk of animal pelt. One of the men brought in a small burner that he placed in the center. He put a small pot on top and soon a foul smell, akin to burnt fish oil, was filling the air.

I closed my eyes.

Outside the tent, the wind was tenaciously tearing at the fabric.

I still couldn't feel my feet, but the palm of my left hand was starting to throb inside its sealskin holster. I attempted to move my fingers, but only succeeded in sending a burning, shooting pain up my arm.

I remained still.

I concentrated on the hushed discussion between the three men.

"We can't go on like this." One of them said in a loud whisper to be heard over the wind. "We're barely making a third of the distance necessary, and today he managed only two hours before collapsing."

"We're close to the depot," Robert replied. "If he rests enough and the wind subsides, I'm hopeful we can get him there."

"I'm not sure it matters anymore," the man called Birdie said. "His stamina is not improving, his feet are in an absolutely wretched condition and he is acutely aware that he is slowing us down. If he could go on, he would, but he simply can't. Remember he asked us to leave him behind yesterday and we wouldn't allow it. He knows his journey has come to an end and we are now the ones holding him back."

"Yet, we are not barbarians, Birdie," said Robert. "I simply won't allow leaving one of our own behind."

"So what do we do? What options do we have?" Wilson asked.

There was a long pause, where none of them spoke and all I could hear was the sound of the tempestuous wind clawing at the surface of the tent.

"We will wait for something to change," Robert finally said.

They halted their conversation and the man called Birdie came to where I lay and gently tapped me on my shoulder. When I opened my eyes, he slid a small rolled up piece of fabric under my head and began to feed me a grainy yet fatty gruel from a small steel bowl. I could have devoured the entire bowl in one mouthful, but he insisted on feeding me slowly and meticulously. The gruel tasted like old dried up meat mixed with stale bread and left a thick, greasy film in my mouth.

I didn't care. In their desperate search for sustenance, my insides were agonizingly ripping at each other and when the small bowl was empty, I felt a pang of despair as deep as I have ever felt.

Birdie held a cup of hot water to my lips and I drank a bit.

My desperate state was reflected in his eyes. However, his wasn't a pitiful stare.

It was a recognition from one man to another that he had done everything in his power to succeed and that, even in defeat, he should be proud of his achievement.

His own face was brutally beaten by the cold. His long narrow curved nose was reddish black and heavily blistered and the skin on his chapped cheekbones was flaking. His face was gaunt, his cheeks hollow, and when he opened his mouth, I noticed the traces of watery blood on his teeth under his cracked lips.

"Do you want me to have a look at your hand?" he asked.

I nodded and he very carefully removed my right glove.

I winced in pain and looked down at my exposed hand.

It was a dreadful sight.

Halfway down to the knuckles, the tips of all four fingers were black as coal. They resembled small pieces of burnt wood. Except, these pieces had fingernails attached and were connected to a puffy hand that had layers of greyish skin detaching from its surface, revealing a blotchy pink complexion underneath. My thumb was sticking out from the hand like a small bulbous branch, the colour of death.

I couldn't bear the sight of the malformation and asked Birdie to cover it.

He nodded and gently slipped the glove back on the mangled limb.

"How are my feet doing?" I asked.

He exchanged glances with Robert and Wilson, who were hunched over a map on the floor, before answering.

"I'll be honest with you," he said, "we checked your feet yesterday, after you collapsed. The toes on your left foot are severely frostbitten and your right foot is now black almost to the ankle." He looked at me. "I'm sorry to tell you this old chap," he said, "but gangrene has set in."

He looked at me and almost imperceptibly shook his head.

I didn't know how to respond to this news, so instead I closed my eyes. He left me to rest and turned to the others to discuss the lack of progress and their thoughts for the upcoming route.

Listening to their conversation, there was no question in my mind that they we were running out of time.

They were under a tremendous amount of physical and mental stress in a most hostile environment.

They all had the telltale signs of serious malnourishment and they were obviously behind schedule.

If they didn't make it to the next depot soon, they would most certainly perish.

As the men settled down for the night, there was not much conversation. They seemed to have exhausted their reserves setting up the tent.

I forced myself to stay awake for as long as possible.

I thought of the raven in Poe's poem and wondered if I was slowly losing my mind as I listened to the repetitious sound of the wind, delivering the same message again and again.

I waited until there was no other sound but the howling wind, before I slowly got up from my bunk.

It took a tremendous amount of effort and I could hardly stomach the pain, but I was finally up. I shuffled over to the entrance of the tent and, using only my left hand, slowly and clumsily undid the ties.

As soon as the ties were undone, the fierce wind seized the canvas and ripped it from my grip. For fear of calling out in pain, I bit into my lip. I could taste the blood on my tongue as my teeth penetrated the parched skin.

I heard a voice behind me. In the roar of the elements, I couldn't be sure which one of them it was.

"Where do you think you are you going?" it said.

"I am just going outside and I may be some time." I said over my shoulder. I exited the tent.

I could hear a voice calling out behind me, as I stumbled into the whiteout. The cold was harrowing and the rapacious wind tore into me without mercy.

I didn't believe I would get very far, but it was of no importance, I had faith that the elements would consume me soon enough.

I walked until I was too exhausted to move. I was near a large drift of ice.

I lay down, rolled over on my back and closed my eyes. This was the moment to finally let go of the pain. I spread out my arms to welcome the great unknown.

I opened my eyes and saw a mysterious creature move in the air above my head.

It was a raven sitting on the hump of a large white bull.

"You are ceasing to exist," it said.

When I opened my eyes, I was lying in the middle of the cold stone floor in the watch room with my arms spread out from my body. I was wearing my overcoat over my pajamas and my untied boots on my naked feet. I had on my hat and my gloves, and my scarf was wrapped tightly around the lower part of my face.

I was, truth be told, bewildered by the dream.
I am, like almost everyone else, familiar with the account of Scott's doomed expedition and I immediately recognized the self-sacrificial act of Captain Oates.

I will not attempt to rationalize this vision, if that is indeed what it is, but attempt to think of it merely as a vivid dream.
It is my apprehensive hypothesis, that I am merely a repository for something infinitely more complex than I can fathom.

He put down the sheet of paper and looked into the distance.

"You are ceasing to exist." He uttered the words and they hovered like a collection of vibrating fragments in the air before dissolving, leaving the room in palpable silence.

He was perplexed by what he had just read.

In his opinion this wasn't a dream, rather it was a recollection of a real episode.

He had of course read the varied accounts of the Antarctic expedition, and the detailed description of the journey from Scott's personal journal. Thus he found what he had just read eerily aberrant. It was almost an exact replication of the events that had taken place on that ill-fated voyage back from the South Pole.

Enoch Soule's recollection didn't make sense. It had too strong a consonance with the real event. It was as if Soule had actually been present on the ice and that he, not Captain Oates, had chosen to leave the tent to disappear in the blizzard.

He got up from his seat.

He looked at the last sentence.

Although he had spoken the words softly, the sound of his voice had penetrated the silence like a pebble thrown into a well.

"Aren't we all?" he said. He lay the sheets down on the table and gazed into space, looking at nothing in particular.

He thought about the selection of words. Somehow it seemed unlikely that Soule would have altered the statements that he had heard in his dreams, and yet he must have been aware of their obvious association. He wondered if the remaining dreams were connected in similar ways. He unraveled the teapot and picked it off the table.

The tea inside was lukewarm, but his scarf was warm. He wrapped it around his neck and carried the pot and the cup downstairs.

He checked his watch. Thirty-five minutes.

He made another pot of tea.

He didn't discard the old leaves, but added a pinch of new ones from the bag. He fished a biscuit out of the tall red cylindrical biscuit tin and waited for the water to boil. As he bit into the biscuit, he thought about what he had read so far.

He didn't know how to decipher the dreams.

Besides the words at the end, he couldn't find any significant similarities between the two stories.

He wondered if Soule's dream about Africa was also somehow based in reality. Yet, how could it be? The inclusion of a talking bull was just too bizarre.

However, he found the way Soule had portrayed the experience in the Antarctic especially unsettling. The description of Oates's demise had been far more ominous inasmuch as it had seemed to be real.

He poured the boiling water into the teapot and filled up the cup as well.

He exchanged the stones and picked up the teapot, the cup and the lamp from the stove.

He automatically counted the twenty-four steps as walked back upstairs.

After he placed the things carefully on the table, he walked over to relieve himself in the fire bucket.

His water left a faint trail of steam in the cold air.

As he let out his water, he looked at the decrepit wall in front of him. One of his predecessors had made quite a delicate carving of a bird sitting on a branch. Both the branch and the bird were fairly generic and it was difficult to tell what kind of bird it was. He reckoned the carving must have been made some time ago, as the crepitating paint had added a fine mottled pattern to the bird's plumage. A sad smile appeared briefly on his face as he recalled his small garden and the chirping sounds of courting birds in the spring.

35

When he finished letting his water he checked the time. Just under ten minutes.

He removed his gloves, grabbed the cup and moved away from the table, before pouring some of the lukewarm water over his right and then his left hand.

When he had washed his hands, he placed the cup on the table and dried his hands thoroughly in his scarf.

He walked over to the window and searched the horizon.

He thought he saw something move close to land to his right.

He held his gaze at the same point until he was certain that there was nothing there. It had probably just been a whale blowing or a larger fish breaking the surface.

He checked the barometer, picked up his logbook and made the first entry of the night, before rewinding the mechanism.

He sat down at the table, picked up the teapot and lightly swirled the liquid. He sat the teapot back down, covered it with his scarf, and pulled his coat tight around his neck. He put on his gloves and held onto the hot stones in his pockets for a while, before reaching for the next sheet of paper.

●

The Cemetery

I was high up in a large tree.

It was nearly dusk and a fine mist was spreading on the ground below. I tightened my grip and looked down to see a pair of scaly black claws holding onto the branch upon which I was sitting. I loosened my grip and lightly jumped. A pair of wings unfolded from my shoulders and flapped cautiously at the air. I settled down on the branch and stretched my wings. They were iridescent black and shone like newly polished gunmetal.

I held on to the branch and felt the air push against me as I forcibly flapped the wings.

I hesitantly jumped to another branch, before I launched and flew into the mist below.

The sensation was most extraordinary. It was as if I was slowly falling against a cushion of air that pressed itself ethereally yet purposefully against me. I instinctively operated my new extremities, glided downward in a large spiral and landed quietly on a tall column.

As far as I could make out in the dwindling light, I was surrounded by a great number of grave markers in an extensive cemetery.

I couldn't see anything move in the twilight, but as I searched the grounds from my vantage point, I noticed a bulky mass lying on a bench not far away.

I flew over to the bench and landed on the top crosspiece.

The iron was cold against my claws.

What had appeared from a distance to be an assortment of discarded clothes, was in fact a man.

He appeared utterly disheveled.

He was sprawled on the bench with one of his limp arms dangling over the edge. His clothes were in shambles. He had dirt on the knees of his black trousers, as if he had been crawling, and his white shirt and ruffled neck tie were both soiled by a variety of stains. A black coat was spread out underneath him and his black shoes were heavily scuffed.

His face was ashen and smeared with dirt.

He had a high and wide forehead and the hollows of his eyes were deep and dark. His receding unruly hair appeared oily, and a modest unkempt mustache sat over a small delicate mouth, from which a stream of pinkish spittle was running down his hollowed cheek.

I observed him for some time.

Due to his waxy complexion and the stillness with which he lay, I presumed him to be dead, but then I heard a distressing rattling sound in the depth of his chest as he laboriously took a breath.

He opened his eyes.

It took some time before his eyes adjusted to the dark, but then he clearly saw me sitting on the top of the bench looking down at him.

He leapt up and pointed a shaky finger in my direction.

"You!" He shouted. "Have I at last ceased to exist in this world? Has your master finally dispatched you to collect my ravaged soul in this caliginous hour?"

After this outburst, he immediately started coughing. He bent over and fumbled for his kerchief in the outer pocket of his coat and covered his mouth while his body was seized by convulsions.

He sat down on the bench contorted in pain.

I waited until his coughing subsided and his wheezing breath slowly returned.

He turned to face me.

"Still, I seem to be clinging onto life in this feculent world," he said through forced breath," so the question is: Are you real, or are you merely a figment of my cerebral malady?"

"I am real," I answered, not thinking how this might affect him.

He instinctively moved to the far end of the bench, and looked at me as if he had encountered a phantasm. His eyes widened and one of his dirty hands flew to his face to hide his open mouth. He stared at me as if struck by horror.

"You spoke," he said at last. "That confirms that I have finally succumbed to my delusions and fully collapsed into madness." He held his head in his hands and began to sob.

"You are not mad," I said, hopping a bit closer on the crosspiece, "I am as real as you are."

He looked up at me with tears streaming down his face.

"That doesn't prove anything," he said sobbing. "The fact that you state that you're as real as me, only proves that my mind is not to be trusted."

He dried his eyes and blew his nose into the kerchief. "However, if my mind somehow projects you as real, what message are you here to convey? What does your master want from me? My soul? Tell him he can have it. It is already beyond repair."

He again buried his head in his hands.

"I am not who you think I am," I answered. "I promise that you have nothing to fear."

"You are wrong," he replied, wrenching his hands in his lap, "fear is bound to me like the kiss of a dead lover. It shall remain forevermore."

"What are you so afraid of?" I asked, cocking my head.

"Everything," he sighed. "Though mostly I fear what may be lying in wait at the end. I am terrified by the mere thought of oblivion."

He dabbed at his brow with the less than clean kerchief.

"Yet I yearn for the end to come," he added after a while. "I have not been feeling well for some time, neither in body nor in mind."

"What are you doing here?" I asked.

"What do you mean?" he replied.

"It's a simple question. What are you doing here alone, so late in the day?"

"I believe that I will soon be dead," he said. "I came to say goodbye to my beloved Virginia and my dear brother Henry. If I shall not have a chance to meet them in the afterlife, I wanted to let them both know how sorry I am to have wronged them in this one."

"What makes you think you are dying?" I asked, ruffling my feathers, jumping a bit closer to where he sat.

"I have a terrible ache inside my head," he said, rubbing at the area just above his right eye. "It feels like my brain continuously presses upon the cranium, as if it wants to escape its bony prison." He kept massaging the area with his thumb, leaving a dirty mark to the right of his brow.

"Also, I have premonitions." He looked at me knowingly. "Just two days ago in Philadelphia, Virginia visited me in my room. She looked so beautiful and altogether halcyon as she stretched out her arms and asked me to join her." He gazed into the approaching darkness, lost in the memory.

"Alas, when I tried to follow her, I walked directly into the sun filled patch on the wall and knocked my head."

He looked at me with a wry smile.

"Despite everything that I have done, I think she still loves me as devotedly as anyone I ever knew." This he said quietly, then he stopped speaking and looked at the ground between his feet.

41

I didn't want to interrupt his apparent reverie, so we sat on the bench in silence.

Suddenly he stood up.

"What's your name?" he asked.

He seemed to no longer recognize the surroundings.

"Are you the conductor?" he asked questioningly. "Is this the train to New York? I am expected in New York shortly, can you please let me know when we get there?"

He then vigorously searched his coat pockets.

"Where is it?" He sounded agitated. "Where is it? Have you seen it?" he asked frantically. "The letter of introduction to Reynolds. Have you seen it? It was here in my pocket only five minutes ago."

He began searching the ground around the bench.

"No, no, no, it can't have disappeared," he cried out.

"It has to be here somewhere." He desperately searched his pockets. When he came up empty handed, he looked behind the nearest marker and began a feverish stumbling search between the gravestones. I heard him falling about in the darkness in his quest to retrieve the lost letter.

As he searched, I flew from column to column to keep him in sight.

After some time, he fell to the ground.

I waited for him to get up, but this time he stayed down.

I flew to where he had fallen and landed near his outstretched arm.

He was lying on his back looking at the stars in the dark expanse above.

"Is there an alternate form of life out there, I wonder?" He didn't wait for my answer, but instead turned his head and looked at me intensely.

"Some time ago I had the strangest dream. Or perhaps it was another hallucination," he said softly.

"These days it has become rather difficult to tell one from the other." He paused briefly. "In any case; I was standing under a large tree in a foreign country. I was alone, but for the company of a large white bull, which was lying on the ground beside me."

There was another pause, before he continued.

"Don't think for a moment, that I don't recognize the irony in telling you this, but the bull spoke to me." He slowly shook his head and closed his fluttering eyelids. "It said that everything, everywhere at some point ceases to exist." He turned his head and looked at the stars. "Although I admit that I didn't fully acknowledge the importance of the dream at the time, I do appreciate it now." He raised his hand and ever so gently ran the tips of his fingers down my feathered back.

"You were always my favorite." He closed his eyes. "However, I don't believe I need you in my life anymore.

When I came to, I was sitting in a hunched position on the floor in the sleeping quarters. My knees and lower legs were close together, pressed against my chest under my chin and my toes were aching on the cold stone floor. My arms were stretched down by my sides and I was completely nude, but for a dark grey blanket wrapped around my shoulders. I do not know how long I had been sitting in the position, but when I finally attempted to stretch my legs, they throbbed as the blood began to flow through my veins, and they continued to prickle for quite some time afterwards.

I was, as you can imagine, very confused and somewhat disturbed by what had just occurred. I believe that I, in the form of a raven, encountered a distressed Mr. Poe at some point late in his life. What is the meaning of this?
How can this be happening? You might ask. The honest answer is: I do not know.

Everything that happens in my sleep, continues to be as great a mystery to me, as it surely must be to you. I am recounting the things that are happening to me, as faithfully as I possibly can and yet I understand how outrageous they must sound.

He put down the sheet.

Like the others, it was light as a feather.

He felt the delicate brush of the fabric against his skin as he carefully placed it on the top of the small pile on the left. He absentmindedly ran his index finger over one of the fairly recent inscriptions in the table's surface. "E" was all it said. There was a small engraved heart next to it.

He checked his watch. Forty minutes.

He walked to the window and stared into the horizon. He thought he saw a small movement in the periphery to his left. He grabbed the binoculars from the hook and scanned the horizon.

He once again kept his gaze at the spot where he'd imagined the movement.

He had been mistaken.

He replaced the binoculars.

He remembered that the raven in Poe's poem had repeatedly uttered the same word 'Nevermore' to the narrator, and that the narrator, already grieving for his dead lover, had driven himself mad by continuously asking the raven questions, to which he already knew the answer.

He was wondering if Poe had meant for the raven to be aware of its actions and if it indeed intended the narrator to lose his mind, or whether the narrator, already driven to madness by grief, had been imagining the raven from the outset.

Whatever the case, he knew that Poe had meant for the raven to be a messenger from the underworld.

He could understand why Poe would have been horrified by the encounter in the cemetery.

However, he couldn't have been. For the simple reason that the encounter had never taken place. It was a merely a figment of an overzealous mind.

Nevertheless, as he gathered up the things from the table, he thought of the image of the raven following the delirious poet through the graveyard like a dark phantom.

He made his way downstairs.

He put the teapot and cup back on the shelf in the cupboard and replaced the stones.

Then he fished out a small pan from the back of the cupboard and put it on the stove. He walked over to the pantry and opened the door. He got out two small tins of beans and put them in his pockets. He then unrolled a small package and removed a thin strip of salted pork, that he held between his teeth, while he rolled up the package, replacing it on the shelf and closing the pantry door.

The door squeaked on its hinges and parts of the flaking paint fell to the ground where they lay like small green pieces of mosaic against the grey floor. He thought it reminded him of something, but he couldn't quite remember what it was.

He put the salted pork in the pot. The pot was quite small and the pork stuck out over the top like a fleshy sprig.

He fished out the can opener from the drawer and removed the tins from his pockets and opened them on the stove top.

He removed the pork from the pan and again held it between his teeth, while he emptied the contents of each can into the pan. He shook them briskly to make sure that they were empty, before discarding them.

They made a metallic clamour as they landed in the waste basket by the stove.

He got out his pocketknife and proceeded to cut little slivers off the sprig of meat. He watched them as they dropped in the pan. He thought they looked like small pink worms on the surface of wet soil.

He finished cutting the pork, put the last piece in his mouth and chewed it, as he looked for a lid.

While he waited he thought of Soule's recent dream.

It was amazing, that the human mind could call forth such

fantastical images.

He had no doubt in Soule's faithful descriptions of his somnambular events. He was after all a lighthouse keeper and as such a level headed man. Furthermore, it was obvious that he took an active part in the narrative and believed himself transformed.

However, he wasn't sure if Soule believed the phenomenon to be dreams or some form of vision or transposed premonition.

As unlikely as it had been for Soule to be present on the ice in the Antarctic, it was equally impossible for him to have encountered the poet, while inhabiting the body of a raven.

Although he was convinced that the dreams were just remarkable intuitive fantasies, there was something about the fact that Soule himself was questioning the substance of the events, that troubled him. He considered whether Soule's mind or his nightly escapades could somehow put him in harm's way. He knew from experience that a simple misstep could have serious implications and that a major misstep could be fatal.

He removed the lid and found the short wooden spoon that he used to stir the food. It wasn't hot yet.

He checked his watch. Twenty-two minutes.

However, he didn't believe that Soule was losing his mind.

As a matter of fact, he found the wording of his descriptions both intelligible and, besides the fancifulness of the narrative, free of mental derangements.

So far Soule seemed to be perfectly lucid when he wrote about what happened to him when he was dreaming; he fully understood how improbable the events would appear to anybody else. The contents of the pan began to simmer and the distinctive aroma of beans filled the room.

He found a dinged white metal bowl with a dark blue rim in the cupboard.

It was cold, so he poured a bit of warm water from the kettle into it. He swished the water around a couple of times and returned it to the kettle. He poured the contents of the pan into the preheated bowl and started eating.

He used the wooden spoon and ate standing up, leaning against the end of the stove.

Even though he ate the same meal at least four or five times a week, he never tired of the repetition.

He genuinely enjoyed the taste and savoured the hot salty tanginess on his tongue.

When he finished eating, he left the bowl and the spoon in the sink, picked up the lamp and the almost empty water bucket and went downstairs. It was dark and damp in the lower regions of the tower and the raw stones looked as if they were perspiring. Their sudoriferous surfaces glistened like a collection of static but living organisms and he quickly refilled the bucket with water from the water reserve and carried it back upstairs.

He checked the time.

Twelve minutes.

He poured some of the water over the dishes in the sink and some into the kettle and put it back on the stove. He then grabbed two of the stones and put them in his pockets and walked back upstairs unwittingly counting the steps.

He closed his hands around the warm stones in his pockets and looked out at the sea.

The night was clear and the enduring fixture of the Big Dipper was hanging, only slightly askew, low in the horizon in the in firmament above.

Although there had been no noticeable change in the weather, he sensed the powerful movement of the ocean beneath him.

It was like a massive untamed beast lying in wait, patiently preparing for the onslaught.

He checked his watch. Three minutes.

He wound up the mechanism and walked to the table, pulled out the chair and sat down.

He picked up a piece of paper from the pile.

The Musician

I was standing opposite a young man, who was sitting cross-legged in the middle of a wooden floor. He was in the center of what I first assumed were the petals of a large elaborate flower, that spread out on the floor around him. However, when I looked closer, I saw that the petals were in fact pieces of paper.

They were of differing sizes and all had words printed on them.

I couldn't see all the way around me, because I was looking out from a peculiar helmet with a dark yet transparent visor. The helmet seemed to be connected to a somewhat bulgy grey uniform that covered the rest of my body. I had on a pair of large grey boots and my hands were enclosed in a pair of enormous grey gloves.

I was in a fairly large room with two massive arched windows. The sun showered the space in a generous benevolent light, in which a cascade of minute particles were floating. Music was playing and I recognized the first movement from the Great Mass in C Minor coming from a record turning on an unusual looking black gramophone, standing on a low dark wooden cabinet.

Next to the gramophone was a large white marble sculpture of Pallas and the Raven. The raven had its neck outstretched and its beak open, silently calling.

I was in fact surrounded by a large number of peculiar objects.

Standing in one corner, there were a couple of odd looking guitars leaning on their stands next to a number of large black boxes with the name Fender and a row of small silver coloured dials at the top. I reckoned they must be some kind of large radios or loudspeakers.

A Moroccan puff and some low pieces of furniture in wood and leather, of a design that I had never before encountered, were placed around a small table that looked like it was made of a thick layer of dark glass. A large crystal ashtray, a package of cigarettes, some small brown packages, a silver spoon and a syringe were turbulently spread across its surface.

There were some large, extremely colourful prints on the walls. A couple of them were merely presenting an arrangement of lines or shapes, others were bizarre smeary portraits of women, conspicuously reminding me of clowns. On my irregular visits to the museum of art, I had never seen anything like it, and I couldn't think of a living artist, who could have produced work such as these.

However, I did recognize a large print of a Campbell's Soup can.

I looked at it for some time and found it odd that somebody would display an advertisement for soup in their home.

I turned to look at the young man in front of me.

He was tall and skinny with long limbs and delicate hands.

He was dressed in a crumpled, loose fitting white shirt, with rolled up sleeves and a pair of deep purple wide cotton pants.

His feet were bare.

His elongated, slightly asymmetrical face had fairly high cheekbones and a straight, rather slim nose. His eyebrows formed a low arch over his large eyes. His full lips downturned at the sides, giving him a somewhat inquiring look, and his wavy blond hair, almost covering his face, was long and unruly.

He gazed in my direction, although I don't believe he actually saw me.

I noticed that his eyes were of different colours.

His left eye appeared much darker than that of the right, which was of a light blue colour, suggestive of the submerged part of an iceberg. I had seen this anomaly in animals before, but never in another human being.

It was curiously mesmerizing.

He kept gazing at me with his dual coloured eyes.

"You are here?" he finally said in a slow baritone voice, when he at last brought me into focus. "When did you arrive?"

"Just now," I said, "were you expecting me?"

"I don't know," he said, pushing his hair behind his ear. "For some reason I've been thinking about you a lot lately and I've just started putting some words together about your trip." He gestured to pieces of paper on the floor around him.

I looked at the words covering the floor and turned my head to read them.

Although it was difficult to ascertain any particular meaning in the chaos, I believe one of the string of words closest to him read:

'I am floating in a most peculiar way' and another to the left of him read: 'planet earth is blue'.

I looked at him.

"Where am I supposed to go?" I asked.

"You don't have a specific destination," he said moving the word 'ground' closer to 'control'. "I think you're just destined to be free from your anxieties on earth."

"But if I have no destination, how can I be free?" I asked. "And where exactly do I go, if I have no destination? Might I not be better off staying right here?"

"I am sure you'll have a very different perspective when you're floating in space," he said smiling.

"Why would I be floating in space?" I asked.

"Because that's where I'm sending you," he replied. He stood up and walked over to the table and picked up the pack of cigarettes. He lit one with a silver lighter that he fished out from his trouser pocket and blew the smoke into the curtain of light, where it hovered aimlessly before slowly dispersing.

He picked up the ashtray and sat back down in the center of the words.

"How do I get up there?" I asked, when he was again sitting on the floor.

"In a spaceship," he said, pulling on the cigarette. "You fly into space and then you leave the spaceship and float away."

"That's not possible," I said. "You can't send people into space. That's merely a fantasy."

"I agree that sending you into space is indeed a fantasy," he said, fiddling with the word 'capsule', that he pushed closer to the word 'dare'. "I'm attempting to bring you to the highest point possible, but keep you connected to earth."

He reached behind him to pick up a small box with a flat shiny surface that he began pressing with a small pin that was attached to the box with a small wire.

A strange haunting sound came out of the box. It was like nothing I have ever heard before, like the sound of a drawn out metallic harpsichord.

The man began humming some of the words in front of him: "I am sitting in a tin can, far above the world. Planet earth is blue...hmmm hmmm."

"Why are you sending me?" I asked. "Are you afraid of taking the trip yourself?"

He stopped humming and looked at me.

"I am taking the trip myself," he said, moving the word 'stars' next to 'different'.

"How can you be taking the trip?" I asked. "Didn't you just say that you're sending me into space to float away?"

The Somnambulist's Dreams

"Yes," he said and looked at me intently, "but I am you, and you are me."

"That cannot be," I said.

"I know better than anybody who you are," he said and moved 'check' next to 'ignition'. "I created you."

"How can I be you then?" I asked irritably.

"That's just the way it is," he answered casually, brushing his hair away from his forehead, picking up the word 'moon'. "We are one and the same."

"I don't believe you," I said, shaking my head. "That's pure madness."

"It might be madness, but that's the way it is." He put 'moon' down next to 'above'.

"I don't understand," I said. "What is the meaning of this?"

"You'll discover that soon enough," he said.

He got up and walked over to the table and knelt down.

He picked up one of the small bags, shook it slightly and poured a fine light brown powder into the silver spoon. He then pulled out the lighter and held the flame underneath the head of the spoon until the spoon turned black and the content inside liquefied and began to froth.

He put the lighter down on the table top and picked up the small syringe. He held the spoon by the very end of its handle, put the needle into the hollow of the spoon and pulled a clear golden liquid into the chamber of the syringe.

He put the spoon and the syringe down on the table and removed a piece of *white cloth from his shirt pocket. He skillfully tied the strip of cloth to his right arm just above the elbow and tightened it by gripping one end of the strip between his fairly large, somewhat uneven, teeth. As he stretched out his arm, I noticed a series of small dark marks near the elbow joint. He opened and closed his hand a couple of times before he carefully inserted the needle into an extended vein in his arm.*

He looked at me while he slowly injected the content of the syringe.

In an all-encompassing deracination I felt an incredibly blinding rush.

The room was suddenly incredibly bright and everything around me subtracted expeditiously, until I was suspended in a vertiginous colourless space.

A man in a peculiar grey outfit was floating in space across from me. He was wearing a helmet with a dark shiny visor. The name tag on the right side of his chest said Major Tom.

I saw my own reflection as I reached out my arms, and with my long delicate hands, slowly lifted the auburn coloured visor and looked at his face.

He had different coloured eyes.

"Do you know who I am?" He asked, before dissolving in a plurality of minuscule flecks.

I was floating in perpetuity.

When I woke up, I was standing in the middle of the watch room with my legs spread out and my arms away from my body. It was very bright in the room and I was wearing my boots and my coveralls and I had my hands in a pair of work gloves. Most peculiarly, one of the large steel bowls from the galley was covering the top my head.

I do not know how to describe what happened to me in the dream or who the young man might have been. I believe he was a poet of some kind or perhaps a musician and certainly an habituated user of diamorphine. However, I have not the slightest idea of who he was. I am not familiar with the words he was singing nor with the sounds he was producing. I am confounded as much by the narrative in the dream, as the images or objects that surrounded me, none of which were familiar.
As to the man in the uniform floating in space, I cannot say. Attempting to explain this supermundane event is beyond my capabilities.

You might think I am losing my mind, however I can assure you, that I am but a receptacle with no command over what is spilled into me.

He put down the page on top of the pile.

He pushed the chair away from the table and stood up. While holding onto his hands, he turned his shoulders and stretched his arms above his head. He ached from the hunched position and he felt a sharp pain somewhere deep in his neck as he rotated the shoulder.

He walked over to the window to perform his natatorial duties.

He gazed into the night and scanned the horizon.

He noticed a slight movement to the right and grabbed the binoculars.

In the clear moonlit night, he could make out the silhouette of a three master schooner bark. He calculated it was about half a nautical mile out. The sea was relatively calm and he didn't believe the schooner was in any trouble.

He watched until it slowly disappeared in the obscurity of the sea. He flipped open his log and noted the description and position of the vessel. He then looked at his watch and added the time to the column on the right. Thirty five minutes until the next rewind.

He put the log back in his pocket and picked up the lamp from the table and made his way downstairs. As he replaced the cold stones on the stove and began the preparations for a fresh pot of tea, he thought of the dream he had just read.

It was unbelievably bizarre.

Although he believed he understood the conversation that had happened between Soule and the young musician, he couldn't fathom the objective. Nor could he make sense of the other individual. What was he supposed to be? Had Soule imagined himself as a spaceman in the body of the young man? And who was Major Tom? It sounded like the ravings of an entirely deluded individual.

When he was young he had of course read the fantastical moon navigation tales by Jules Verne and The War of the Worlds by H. G. Wells. He was also familiar with the tales of travel into space and had once, long ago, watched the movie A Trip to the Moon in the movie theater.

However, he had never heard of anybody flying into space, leaving their spaceship and floating away in space. Surely this was undeniable proof that Soule's dreams were mere fantasies produced by an increasingly unbalanced mind.

He scratched his head and looked at the white painted walls while he waited for the water to boil. This coming spring he had to repaint the outside of the tower. The two red warning stripes were bleached by the constant onslaught of the elements and the white paint had etiolated so much that the original stone shone through underneath. In a couple of years he would probably have to do the inside as well. He looked at the cracks in the plastered ceiling above and sighed.

He checked his watch. Twenty two minutes.

He was wondering what had happened when the young man had injected himself with the narcotic substance. The way that Soule had described it, it was as if he himself had had a euphoric episode in his dream state, much like he had been dreaming in his dream. It also seemed like he had experienced, not only a reversal of the self of the spaceman and the young musician, but concurrently a singularity of the two.

He ran his forefinger and thumb across his brow.

He found the thought of that impossible.

There was no question, that Soule was imagining all of these events and yet he continued to describe them as if he believed that they were not the fabrication of a miasmatic mind, but somehow connected to reality.

He wondered if it was possible that Soule's dreams were correlated to the real world.

"I must be mad as a March hare to even consider that," he said, shaking his head in puzzlement.

He cleaned out the old tea leaves and washed the cup in the cold water in the sink and put it on the end of the stove.

The water began to boil and he poured a little into the cold teapot and cup and swirled it about, before making the second pot of tea of the night.

He picked up two of the stones and put them in his pockets. He then adeptly lifted the teapot and the cup with one hand, and the lamp with the other, and walked back upstairs.

He put the teapot and the cup down on the table, wrapped the teapot in the scarf and pulled his coat close around his neck. He looked at the watch and closed the cover. There was a dull metallic click as the lock connected. Six minutes.

He stood by the window and looked at the sea, while gently clutching the warm stones in his pockets.

He wound up the mechanism and slowly scanned the horizon before he walked over to the table and sat down.

He lifted the teapot and gently swirled the liquid around inside, before setting the pot back down on the table and covering it with his scarf.

He rubbed his hands together and picked up a sheet of paper from the diminishing pile on the right.

The Well

I was sitting with my back up against the wall in the bottom of a well. The ground around me was dry and sandy. I reached out and picked up a handful of sand. As it flowed between the gaps in my fingers, it created a small curtain of particles in the air. I brushed my hand against my trouser leg and looked up at the opening above me.

All I could see was a cloudy ceiling.

I looked at the lead grey stones and wondered what I was doing in an old well.

I stood up.

I was wearing a pair of sand coloured trousers, a light blue short sleeved shirt with white semi opaque buttons and a pair of brown sandals on my wide bare feet.

There was a dark brown leather bag on the floor next to me.

When I looked inside, I found a small black box filled with unfamiliar food and a canteen with a hot liquid that had a salty and tangy aroma. I screwed the lid back on the canteen and put it back in the bag.

I stretched my arms and turned around, touching the walls around me.

The well was nearly symmetrical. It was obvious that it had been constructed by somebody who knew what they were doing. I lay down on the ground.

When the top of my head was pressed up against the wall, I couldn't fully stretch my legs.

The clouds moved slowly in the sky above.

I asked myself if somebody might have put me in the well, but I couldn't imagine why. Also, there was a small rope ladder hanging down from the top, so if somebody had put me in here, they had not meant for me to be imprisoned.

It was a much more likely scenario, that I had climbed into the well on my own.

I thought that I might have been looking for something and began to scoop up handfuls of sand from the ground searching the granules.

After a while I gave up the search, having found nothing but sand.

Instead I thought about some of the reasons I might have crawled into the well. Perhaps I was hiding from somebody.

When I sat back down, I felt something in my back pocket. I reached behind me and removed a small black notebook with rounded corners. It had no distinguishing marks on the front or the back.

I opened it.

It was filled with characters that looked Japanese. There were hundreds of them, all drawn neatly in tight rows. I flipped through the pages, but nothing was written in a language I could understand.

The only familiar thing I found was a small drawing of a sitting cat in the margin of one of the pages.

When I moved it close to my eyes, it looked like the cat had the markings of a bird on its side.

Perhaps the cat might have something to do with me being in the well. If the cat was mine, it was possible that I had come down here to look for it.

I looked around. There were no signs of a cat.

I leant back against the rounded wall and looked up.

I was staring at the clouds slowly drifting by, when I noticed something moving at the top of the well.

I put my hand over my eyes to shield them against the light.

It looked like a bird was sitting on the edge of the well.

It turned its head from one side to the other, peering down at me inquisitively .

A short while later, it spread its wings and silently dove down the well shaft. It stayed clear of the walls and landed softly on the leather bag.

When it had been sitting at the top of the well, I thought the bird was a seagull. Now that it was only a couple of feet away from me, I realized it was a white raven. It shifted its position on the bag and looked at me with its head at a slight angle.

I noticed it had different coloured eyes.

Its left eye was the boundless colour of obsidian and its right was a lustrous crystalline blue.

As it stared at me, first with one, then the other eye, I couldn't help but feel that I was being assessed.

The raven sat for a while inspecting me, as if it was deliberating its next step.

"Who are you?" it asked in a smooth low voice.

I was completely taken aback. I wondered if I had imagined the sound, as I stared at the bird dumbfounded.

"Who are you?" it asked again. "You are obviously not Toru, so you must be someone else. So, the question is: Who are you?" It shifted its position on the bag.

"My name is Enoch Soule." I replied, after I had recovered my senses. "I am a lighthouse keeper."

"This is an ironic place for a lighthouse keeper to be, don't you think?" The raven looked around. "Are you sure you are telling the truth?"

"Yes, I'm telling the truth."

"Just checking," the raven said, jumping on the bag.

"Who are you?" I asked.

"I am a raven."

"I can see that," I said. "What's your name?"

"Nevermore," It answered, and looked at me with its obsidian eye.

It must have noticed my obvious skepticism.

"Only joking," it said, "my real name is Tom."

" Tom? That's a peculiar name for a raven," I said. "Who named you?"

"That has always been my name." The raven ruffled its back feathers.

"What are you doing here?" It asked.

"I was thinking about that before you arrived," I replied. "I might be in here looking for something, but the truth is, I don't really know. I don't even know how I got here."

"When I first met Toru, he told me he was looking for his cat," the raven said, "However, he enjoys being down here. I believe it's his way of escaping the drudgery of reality and at the same time creating a bit of mystery in his life. He's been coming here for quite some time you know." He looked at me with his icy blue eye.

"I don't know anyone named Toru," I said. "Who is he?"

"He's the guy looking for the cat."

"Yes, you said that already, but who is he?" I asked.

"Just a guy looking for a cat, that he seems to be unable to find," the raven replied.

"What is his profession?" I asked. "He must be doing something with his life, besides coming down this well?"

"At this moment it's of no importance what else he is doing in his life," the raven said. "The important thing is that he's still looking for his cat."

"What are you doing here?" I asked, when I realized I wasn't getting closer to the identity of Toru.

"Having a conversation with you," it answered. "Although, sometimes I merely listen."

"What do you listen to?"

"I'll give you an example," it said. "Not too long ago, I was sitting in the crown of a large tree. On the ground below me, a man and a bull were talking about the meaning and interpretations of words. At first, I wasn't paying any particular attention to their conversation, but then a woman arrived. She asked the man why he was there, and he explained to her that the bull was dying. I could sense that she became overwhelmed with a profound sadness and as she touched the bull with her hand, everything dissolved into nothingness." The raven looked at me inquisitively.

"What does that mean?" I asked.

"I'm not sure," it said , "but, I suspect I was there because I needed to listen to their conversation. Also, the man talking to the bull was not who he seemed to be."

"Who was he?" I asked.

"He said his name was the same as yours. Enoch Soule."

"That's preposterous," I said. "I have never had a conversation with a bull about the interpretations of words. That's pure nonsense."

"So you've had conversations with bulls about other things?" The raven cocked its head.

"That's not what I said," I replied, "I said the notion of having a

conversation with a bull was absurd."

"Yet, here you are, sitting in the bottom of a well having a discussion about the absurdity of that with me, while inhabiting the body of another person."

The raven shook its head and jumped around on the bag.

"Do you have a particular liking for the paradoxical?"

"What is the meaning of this?" I asked. "Is this an attempt to question my sanity?" I rubbed my chin, which was clean shaven and remarkably smooth.

"I don't know," it said, "are you sane?"

"Until your arrival here, I would have given you a resounding yes. However, now I'm not so sure." I scratched the side of my head, noticing the hair was a bit shorter and coarser than my own.

"Not to change the subject," said the raven, "but I'm hungry. What's for lunch?"

It jumped down from the bag.

I reached over, picked up the bag and took out the small black box and the canteen. I placed the steel canteen on the ground beside me.

I opened the lid of the box to reveal the strange looking food. There were three compartments in the bottom of the box. In the larger compartment were eight small parcels of rice, each with a piece of pink raw fish on top. They all had a thin dark band of an unusual material wrapped around them.

In one of the small compartments, there were some peculiar looking stringy green vegetables and some thinly cut disks, that looked like tiny onions. A couple of small white packets were lying in the bottom of the last compartment.

"Mmmm," said the raven, "Toru knows I love Nigiri sushi." It jumped over and grabbed one of the small parcels from the box. It held the parcel in its beak for a moment, then he threw it into the air, much like a seagull would a fish, caught it again and swallowed it in one bite.

The raven looked at me.

"You can pour some of the miso into the lid of the thermos," it indicated with its head the canteen next to me. "But please swirl it first," it added, when I picked up the canteen to unscrew the lid.

"It's important that the miso is homogeneous when you drink it." It watched as I poured some of the liquid into the lid of the canteen.

It smelled faintly of the sea.

I lifted the lid to my mouth and sipped at the edge. The taste was far from unpleasant. It wasn't like tea at all; it tasted salty and sweet with a somewhat earthy aftertaste.

"What is this?" I asked.

"It's miso soup," answered the raven. "Toru told me it's made from fermented soybeans. It's good isn't it?" I tilted the cup slightly as the raven put its beak in the lid to drink.

"You should try the Nigiri and the pickles as well," it said, grabbing another parcel of rice and fish, that it flung into the air and expertly caught, before swallowing.

"You can open one of these and dip the Nigiri in soy sauce if you want."

The raven said and picked up one of the small white packets.

I ripped the edge and a thin inky liquid poured into one of the smaller sections of the box. I dipped my finger and tasted it. It was not dissimilar to the miso soup, but much saltier.

"What's that?" I asked, pointing at the small dark band around the parcel.

"Nori, It's dried seaweed. It doesn't really taste of much, but I suppose it adds texture."

I picked up one of the pieces of Nigiri and dipped it in the soy sauce before putting the entire piece in my mouth.

The raw fish was soft with a delicate fishy taste and the ball of rice was somewhat viscous, but the combined taste was delightful.

I found myself quite enjoying this unexpected lunch.

"Let's talk about why you are here," the raven said, looking at me from his perch.

"I already told you, I don't know," I said, chewing on some of the pickled seaweed.

"Don't you find it particularly idiosyncratic that you, as the keeper of a lighthouse, are sitting at the bottom of a well? Surely you must have asked

yourself why, of all the places in the world, you have ended up here." The raven gazed at me with its obsidian eye.

"Yes, of course I have. I just can't come up with a possible explanation. As I said earlier, perhaps I am in here searching for something. Although, I'm still not sure what that might be." I looked at the raven, who turned its head and stared at me with its sapphire blue eye.

"Why do you think I'm here?" I asked. "You seem to be well informed as to my alleged whereabouts."

"I can't tell you why you are present. You are the only one who can do that. I can however tell you that you are present." It spread its wings and flapped them lightly in the stale air.

"What's that supposed to mean?" I said. "That I'm here?"

"Yes," it said "that's exactly what it means. That you are here."

"But why?" I asked.

"That's what I just asked you."

"But I don't know why I'm here," I said, irritated. "Or indeed why I would have been anywhere else you might have encountered me."

"I didn't say I encountered you. I merely said that I overheard somebody saying he was Enoch Soule." The raven looked at me quizzically.

I stared back.

"Who are you?" I asked.

"I am Tom," it replied.

"Yes, you said so, but what is your purpose? Why are you here?" I asked.

"I am here talking to you."

"Why? What is it that you want to talk to me about?"

"Whatever you want to talk about," it said.

"I want to talk about why you are here."

"I am here because you are present," it answered.

"That doesn't explain anything," I said. "You said you come here to visit Toru. He is not here, I am. Saying that you are here, because I am present is erroneous."

"It is not," said the raven. "You believe you are here because you are searching for something. I am here to assist you."

"How can you assist me, if I don't know what I am looking for?"

"Hopefully I'm not the first to tell you this: Nothing is ever what it seems. Perhaps you have been asking yourself a sophistical question from the beginning. Maybe it is not about what you are searching for, but what you have already found."

"That's merely another gelastic statement, It doesn't prove or disprove anything."

"It proves that you are present in this well and that you have indeed found something." The raven ruffled its feathers.

"That's a feeble argument," I said. "Even though I don't know what I am looking for, I would always find something."

"Exactly," it said, pulling at a primary wing feather with its beak.

For a while we were sitting in silence.

The raven kept pruning its feathers.

I looked at the clouds above. They were still moving slowly across the sky.

"Can I ask you a question?" said the raven.

"Of course," I replied.

"Where do you think you are?"

"I don't know," I responded. "Where do you think I am?"

"I can't tell you more than you already know, but I can show you something." The raven jumped down on the ground and used its claw to draw a circle in the sand. It was about half a foot across and remarkably symmetrical.

"It's a circle," I said.

"Yes it is," it replied.

"Is that supposed to tell me something? It's a circle drawn in the sand of a dry well."

"That's a matter of perspective." The raven looked at me with his melanoid eye.

I stared back at it.

I noticed that the iris was the colour of dark wet clay and the pupil was the colour of onyx. Where they connected, I could just make out a minuscule golden circle. As I gazed at it, the pupil expanded. I thought I caught a glimpse of tiny pinpricks of lights inside. As I leant closer, the pupil

expanded even further and I had the sensation that the ground and the wall

of the well disintegrated and began to move away from me.

The raven disappeared and I was suspended in an illimitable space,

surrounded by a profusion of stars and cloud formations in colours I could

have never imagined. My hands left a trail of atomic particles behind, when

I moved them to open the visor on my helmet.

When I woke up, I was sitting with my back against the pantry in the galley. I was wearing my pajamas, and my bag and my logbook were lying on the floor next to me. I was holding a half-eaten piece of kipper in my left hand and I had a salty fishy taste in my mouth. I picked up my log and flipped through the pages. On the second to last page, I found a drawing of a small cat in the margin. It was sitting down and had the outline of a bird marked on its side.

As I have already stated, it is impossible for me to decode the narrative of these dreams. However, it must suffice to mention, that my latest dream is connected to the other events. Why? I do not know.

The dreams are truly enigmatic, but I am still at a complete loss to their meaning. No matter how preposterous they sound when I write them down, I can assure you I am not fantasizing. I can only promise that what I am telling you is a truthful account of the events. I am not losing my mind.

He put down the sheet he was holding and gazed into the distance.

After a while he slowly got up from the chair. His backside was sore and began tingling as he walked over to the window.

As he looked into the night, he rubbed at his upper legs and his posterior to get the blood flowing again.

Besides the rolling of the sea, nothing moved. He looked up into the infinite expanse above and wondered what it would be like to be floating in the empyrean space. Would earth become another minute puncture in the fabric of space? A tiny light in the crepuscule?

He checked his watch. Thirty five minutes.

He walked back across the floor and picked up the scarf and wrapped it around his neck.

It was warm.

He picked up the teapot, the cup and the lamp from the table and made his way downstairs.

He put down the pot and the cup at the end of the stove, fished out the stones from his pockets and placed them next to the other two. He then lifted the kettle, checked the amount of water, and put it back down in the center of the stove. He took of the lid of the teapot, got out the bag from the cupboard, opened it and pinched a small amount of leaves between his fingers and added them to the lukewarm tea in the bottom of the pot.

He looked as the dry leaves floated on top of the dark liquid. They slowly spiraled on the surface before they became saturated and languidly descended to the bottom.

He thought about what he had just read.

Although he believed he understood the conversation between Soule and the raven, he didn't know how to make sense of the individual elements.

He found the overall narrative incredibly bewildering and each individual story only added to the general ambiguity.

Soule obviously believed that he had inhabited the body of a Japanese man, who, for nebulous reasons, had crawled into a well, and that he had been sharing a strange lunch with a white raven who bizarrely had resembled the young addict in the previous story.

What happened after that he found beyond incomprehensible.

If he hadn't read Soule's rational descriptions of the events, he would have said that they were undeniably the ravings of a derailed mind. Though he did wonder if Soule himself was fearful of losing his sanity, he was still of the opinion that he, although a fantasist when sleepwalking, was honest in his depictions.

However, it became increasingly difficult to believe that Soule's mind was not somehow affected by these fantastical tales.

He closed his eyes and scratched both sides of his head with his hands.

The fact that the raven had also been present in the African tale and had listened to the conversation between Soule and the bull also confused him. Why had it been there? What was it trying to learn?

That Soule's dreams were not communicating his own experiences was clear. He wondered for a moment if the individual fragments could somehow be a manifestation of Soule's personal vision and made explicit in his dreams, but quickly dismissed it. From reading his descriptions he very much doubted that Soule was capable of such a feat. It was much more likely that these events were brought into existence fortuitously.

The water boiled.

He picked up the kettle and poured most of the water into the teapot and a little into the cup.

Although they shared a profession, he was thinking about how ordinary his own life seemed to be in comparison to Soule's. Although he didn't actively seek these visions, and despite the underlying predicament they might symbolize, Soule's nightly apparitions at least presented him with adventure and excitement, however bizarre the narrative.

He stared at the teapot.

He wondered how many times he filled, emptied and refilled it each day? How many times a day did he count the steps to walk up and gaze out at the sea? How many times had he checked the time on his watch? How many times had he wound up the mechanism?

He wondered if the habitual pattern of his daily activities was the only thing that gave meaning to his life.

He fished the watch out of his pocket. Twelve minutes.

He walked over to the pantry, opened the door and grabbed the box of Graham crackers from the shelf. He removed two crackers from the box, closed the lid and replaced the box.

He shut the door to the pantry and walked back to the stove where he picked up two hot stones and slipped them into his pockets.

He then emptied the cup in the kettle, picked up the teapot and the lamp and went back upstairs.

He put the teapot, cup and lamp carefully down in the corner of the table.

He took off his scarf and wrapped it around the teapot.

While he looked into the night, slowly scanning the horizon, he reached into his pockets. He lightly stroked the stones with his fingertips and felt a small twinge in his heart from the warm smooth surface.

He checked the time.

Four minutes.

He walked over and wound up the mechanism and counted the revolutions. He stopped winding when he could feel the resistance in the weights.

As he walked back to the table he checked the time.

He put his watch back in his pocket, pulled out the chair and sat down.

He picked up the teapot and swirled the tea within. He waited for the leaves to settle before pouring a small amount of fairly weak tea into his cup. He put the teapot down, lifted the cup to his lips and blew on the hot liquid before sipping a bit of the tea. It needed to stew some more.

He put down the cup and picked up a new sheet from the pile.

The Chess Player

I was in a fairly large room.

Darkness loomed outside the lone window and the room was lit by a single lamp hanging from the ceiling high above.

I looked down.

A pair of black scaly claws were holding onto the back of a high backed wooden chair. I jumped a couple of times and gently flapped my wings in the air. They were the colour of coal.

I folded them, tucked them close to my body and surveyed the room.

There were a number of strange objects in the space around me.

What looked like a collection of sugar cubes, trapped in a tiny cage, were sitting on a teak sideboard by the wall next to couple of small bronze sculptures. One of them resembled a leaf lying on a small acclivity and the other an elongated handle of sorts.

On a tall white stool next to me, a black bicycle wheel had been placed upside down, so that the neck of the fork was penetrating the seat of the stool. In the distance, cutting the room in half, a centrally placed large frame had paper cutouts between large sheets of glass.

Most disturbingly, I thought at first a dead nude woman was lying in some brush next to a painting of a landscape at the end of the space. However, when I looked closer, I realized it was a life size female doll, holding what looked like a small lamp in her hand.

There were a multitude of photographs, drawings and paintings displayed on the walls, all of which were as strange in appearance as the objects. One of the photographs was the image of a sitting nude woman with the drawings of the F-hole of a string instrument on her back.

I must admit I was somewhat flummoxed by the collection of images around me and certainly by the candid nature of the motifs.

Although I had never seen work like it before, I presumed that I was in the studio of an artist or perhaps a very eccentric art collector.

In front of me, underneath a small steel lamp shade in the shape of an upside down bullet, was a fairly sizable table. An impressive wooden chess set was sitting in the middle and the pieces were positioned as if they were in play.

The chess pieces were not of a design with which I was familiar. They were asymmetrical and quite outlandish looking and although I am a reasonably seasoned chess player, it was difficult for me to tell them apart.

Both the pieces and the board looked like they were carved from Ebony and Maple and the shadows cast from the large pieces fell on the checkered pattern, creating a series of narrow recondite bridges between them.

As far as I could see, I was occupying the white side of the board.

On the other side of the table an old man sat on a wooden chair not dissimilar to the one upon which I was currently resting. He was smoking a pipe and his features were briefly hidden in the haze of smoke. He was so quiet I thought he might be dozing, but then he leaned forward in his seat and looked at me through the haze.

He was tall and rawboned, dressed in a black sweater over a tattered black and white plaid shirt.

His gaunt face was elongated and furrowed, like time itself had carved an effigy of linear events into his skin.

His ears were large and fleshy and his thin hair had receded to the top of his skull. The skin under his eyes was slack and his dark eyes were lying deep in their sockets.

His long prominent nose, high cheekbones and a cuspate chin, gave him the appearance of a large raptor. As he leaned forward to gaze at me his thin lips were pressed around the black mouthpiece of a pipe.

He removed the pipe and held its glowing wooden head in his long bony fingers.

"Nevermore," he said, "you have finally arrived, and if I say so myself, not a moment too soon." He spoke in a mellow not too deep voice with a trace of an accent I couldn't decipher.

He drew on his pipe and blew out a cloud of smoke that thickly enveloped the air in front of him, where it curled its wispy limbs around itself before slowly dissipating.

His pipe emitted a hazy wavy blanket into the air.

"I am not who you think I am," I said.

The old man looked at me through the haze. I don't know what I had expected, but he didn't seem at all surprised by the announcement. He just kept staring at me with his head at a slight angle.

Finally he removed his pipe and used the black stem to point at me.

"Who are you then?" he asked. "Are you Huginn or Muninn coming to check on my impending demise, so you can report back to your master?" He looked at me with interest. "I must say I very much appreciate the idea." He paused briefly. "Although, thinking about it, it is highly unlikely that Odin would be interested in the wellbeing of an ancient chess player."

He again drew on his pipe and released another billow of smoke in the air.

"However, as I am not currently aware of any other ravens that are capable of human speech, I must assume you are one of the two. That is, if you are not Nevermore."

He looked at me questioningly.

"So which one are you?" he asked. "Huginn or Muninn?"

"Neither," I said, "Nor am I the raven from Poe's poem. My name is Enoch Soule and I am a lighthouse keeper." I jumped from one end of the chair to the other.

"Enoch Soule," he said with quite the emphasis, " that's a most felicitous name for a black raven, don't you think?" The old man smiled. "A man who apparently didn't die, joined with the word that is a close parallel to *the ultimate essence of mankind."*

He slowly nodded his head. "I couldn't have thought of a more becoming name myself, even if I'd tried."

He looked at me approvingly.

"I have never really thought about my name like that," I replied.

"Who named you?" he asked through his teeth, before letting out another plume.

"My mother and father of course," I answered.

"Did they name you when you were a chick or a boy?" the old man asked, clearly amused by his own wit.

"As a boy of course," I said, and ruffled my feathers. "This is not my regular form."

"They must have had high hopes for you, bestowing you with a name like that. Or perhaps they were already aware of your destiny. Whatever the case, Enoch Soule is positively the most excellent name for you." He looked at me and chuckled.

"I was not aware that my name had a hidden meaning," I said. "I always thought it was just a name."

"Nothing is ever what it seems." The old man blew another plume of smoke into the air.

"So what are you doing here Soule?" he asked, picking up a thin white porcelain cup from a small low table next to his chair. He took a sip and

looked at me over the edge. "You must have a good reason to show up at an old man's studio late at night. Or maybe you came to play a game of chess?"

He smiled and his eyes twinkled in the dark.

"I honestly don't know why I am here," I said. "Although, I doubt that I am here to play chess. Perhaps I am here, because you have something to reveal."

"You are putting a lot of pressure on an old man." He put his cup back on the table.

"So what do you want to talk about?" he asked, still smiling.

"I don't really know," I said, shaking my tail. "Why don't you tell me what are you doing here so late at night."

"Ok," he said, leaning back in his chair. "Most of the time I'm asleep in my chair. When I'm not sleeping, I'm playing chess and when I'm not playing chess, I'm thinking."

"What do you think about?" I asked, turning my head to the left.

"Oh, it used to be about this and that, but these days it's mainly about chess or sleeping." He chuckled again, obviously happy with his witty reply.

"How can you play chess against yourself?" I asked. "Does that not defy the purpose of the game?"

"Initially you might think so, but I quite like to keep my mind occupied and the reality is that there are a lot of commonalities between chess and a lot of

the things I used to do." He gestured to the objects in the space behind me.

I jumped around on my chair and looked at them.

"You made all of these?" I asked. "Why?

"That is an excellent question Soule," he said, shaking his head. "A most

excellent question, to which I do not yet have a satisfactory answer."

He picked up the cup and took a sip, before replacing it. He stuck the pipe

back in his mouth and I could hear a muffled clatter as he clenched at the

black mouthpiece with his teeth.

"If truth be told, I find that there are quite a lot of commonalities between

a game of chess and the work that I have spent many years producing.

When you are playing a game of chess, it's very much like you are

constructing something greater. It is not merely about the position of

individual pieces, it's essentially about the overall design." He was clearly

warming to the subject. "The winning or losing is of absolutely no

importance, but the game itself is very plastic. It moves in an expanse,

which is no longer ruled by time and space, where it loses its cardinal

meaning and becomes an illimitable number of varying sequences."

He looked at me.

"Do you follow?" he asked politely.

"I believe so," I replied.

"In many ways, the work I have produced over the last couple of decades

share the same theoretical foundation. An object is always influenced by the context in which it is situated and every time an object is moved or something is added to its situation, one is essentially forced to reanalyze its position."

He paused briefly and looked at me through the smoky air, then continued.

"I play against myself, because that way I can be completely unbiased. In continuously shifting my perspective from white to black and back again, I am not trying to force one upon the other, but to join two opposing creative elements into one combinational realm."

He blew another plume of smoke into the air and watched it as it slowly swirled upwards towards the light, where it drifted aimlessly before dissolving.

"There is no winning or losing, only the eternal plasticity of the game itself."

He removed his pipe and smiled in my direction.

"Nevertheless, isn't it somewhat frustrating playing against yourself?"

"Not at all," he said, then briefly paused. "When you remove the element of victory, there simply isn't a psychological or territorial conflict between the opposing sides. They are no longer dissonant. They are merely a collection of individual elements occupying the same domain, like smaller fragments in a much larger ecumenical whole."

He sat back in his chair and his face almost disappeared in the shadows, behind the hazy curtain of smoke from his pipe.

"It is really no different than the colour of your eyes," he said from the shadows. "One is light, the other dark and yet they operate ceaselessly within the same system."

His bony hand, holding the head of the pipe, moved into the light. The tips of his fingers were nicotine stained and his thumb was smudged by the ashes from the glowing pipe.

"You are aware that your left eye is pearly blue and your right eye is as dark as the bottom of a well?" he asked, leaning forward in his chair.

"No," I answered, "I can't say that I was." I flapped my wings in the air and briefly lifted my claws from the back of the chair, before settling down again. "As far as I know, they function as well as each other." I looked at him first with one then the other eye.

"Perhaps the colours of your eyes is just an exceptional coincidence or it is an essential part of your anomalistic arrival here," he said after a while.

"I do begin to wonder whether your being here is an exhortation." He looked at the smoke snaking its way out of the bowl of his pipe.

"Although, it could be entirely the other way around." He looked at me with intensity. "Perhaps you didn't arrive here, so I could reveal something to you. Perhaps you are here to reveal something to me."

He paused and gazed at me for what seemed like quite a long time.

"So what is it Enoch Soule? Why are you here? What are you here to tell me?" He looked at me expectantly.

"I honestly don't know," I said, shaking my head. " I don't believe I have anything profound to reveal."

I hopped around on the back of the chair.

"Ceci n'est pas une pipe," he said, and looked at me inquisitively.

"Everything is never what it seems, but sometimes what you see, is so obvious that you cannot make sense of it."

He removed the pipe from his mouth and smiled.

"A long time ago, when I was a much younger man, I had a dream," he said softly. "I dreamt that I was hovering or gliding in the air over a graveyard and although I couldn't feel it, I knew it was cold,

because I could see my breath like small puffs of smoke in the air.

It was early evening and I was circling the air for quite a while, before I noticed a man lying on the ground."

He paused for a moment as if to recollect the event.

"He was alone, but for the company of a black raven sitting next to him. I thought at first that he was dead, but then I heard him speak quietly to the bird. From where I was hovering, his voice was faint and I couldn't make out what he was saying."

He blew a cloud of smoke into the already silvery air.

"After a while, he stopped talking. Then he slowly reached out his hand towards the raven, but as soon as his fingers made contact, everything dissolved and I woke up."

He picked up his cup from the side table and brought it to his lips.

He replaced it and leant back in his chair, once again disappearing in the shadows.

"I only had that dream once and always thought of it as an omen, but now I believe everything has fallen into place."

He reached out his hand and his long bony fingers seized one of the dark chess pieces. As he moved it diagonally across the board, the light above began to flicker.

He let go of the piece.

As he did so the light went out, leaving us in darkness.

"I know why you are here," he said.

I woke up in the galley.

I was crouched, back to front on a chair with my knees on my chest. I was completely in the nude, except for an old grey blanket that was wrapped around my shoulders. The blanket was hanging down on either side of me, covering my arms, that were tucked close to my body.

My legs and feet were numb under the weight of my body. I do not know for how long I had been sitting in this position, but when I attempted to stretch my legs, it felt like thousands of tiny ants biting me on the inside. I feel off the chair and landed heavily on the stone floor.

My legs were useless and both my knees hurt from the impact. I lay on the cold floor until I could again move my legs and slowly got up to a standing position.

I do not know what to make of the dream.

I do not know who I, in the form of a raven, had just been visiting. I have never encountered this man before and have certainly never laid eyes on any of the unrepresentative images and objects that surrounded me.

Although you might expect from their description that they were the work of a debauched and licentious soul, I do not believe that to be the case. When truth be told, I found most of them strangely fascinating and some of them even quite beautiful.

I do not endeavour to speculate what the chess player realized just before I awoke. Your guess is equally as good as mine. As I have repeatedly stated, my dreams continue to be great a mystery to me and although they may sound outrageous, I promise you that I am writing down what is happening as truthfully as I possibly can.

He lay the sheet of paper on top of the pile on the left.

After a while he stood up and stretched his arms over his head, then he reached down to unravel the scarf from the teapot to wrap it around his neck.

It felt soft and warm against his skin.

He fished out his watch from his pocket and flipped open the cover.

Forty two minutes.

He shut the cover and pressed down until he heard the satisfying dull click of the lock.

He walked over to the window, looked out at the sea and methodically scanned the horizon.

The waves were quietly oscillating and only the occasional spray broke the aqueous leaden surface.

He looked up at the stars and while searching his inside pocket for his pipe and tobacco, he thought about what he had just read.

He had recognized one of the pieces described in the dream.

He was certain he had read about the bicycle wheel on the stool somewhere. He believed the artist to be from Europe, but he found it difficult to remember from which country or indeed the name of the artist.

He scratched his head with one of his hands, while locating the pipe and the tobacco with the other.

Reading about someone else smoking, had promptly inspired him to find his own pipe.

He pulled out his pouch and the pipe from one of his many coat pockets. He would have preferred to have kept the tobacco in its original packaging, mainly because he appreciated the overall design and enjoyed the silver tongued name Evening Stroll.

He had, however, found the can too cumbersome to carry around, so now he regularly opted for the pouch.

He sat down on the chair and tapped the head of the pipe against the heel of his shoe. His favorite pipe was a much used, dark briarroot with a fairly small straight head. As he gently tapped it, a few curls of unsmoked tobacco fell out with the ashes. He looked at the discarded remains on the floor, as he put the head of the pipe in the pouch and stuffed the bowl with fresh tobacco.

When he felt an adequate amount of springy resistance from the moist tobacco, he put the pouch back in his pocket and patted his coat in search for matches. When he couldn't find them, he stuck the cold pipe between his teeth, got up and collected the teapot, cup and lamp from the table and walked downstairs.

He replaced the cup and teapot on the stove and carried the lamp to the cupboard, where he opened the door and let his free hand search the top shelf for a box of matches.

After hauling out a piece of tarnished string and grimy spool of black thread, he found one tucked away at the very back and caught it between his index and middle finger.

He put the lamp down and lit a match and brought it to the bowl of the pipe. As he sucked in the air, the flame impulsively buried itself between the strands of tobacco. He gazed at the glowing snakes expanding and contracting in the center of bowl, while the smoke twirled in thick bands around him.

When the pipe was properly lit, he blew a plume of smoke into the air and shook his hand, both to disperse the smoke and to extinguish the match.

The tobacco was mellow and sweet on his tongue and he savoured the taste.

He thought about Soule's dream.

He wondered if the raven in the dream was indeed an omen. Although It was no trouble for him to cast the raven in the role of the obligatory conveyor of death, he was nonetheless hesitant to do so. It somehow didn't fit the general account of Soule's expanding dreamscape.

He looked at the smoke hazily filling the galley. He held the lip of the pipe between his teeth while he used both hands to pick out the two cold stones from his pockets.

He replaced them on the stove and checked his watch. Twenty four minutes.

Before putting the kettle back on the stove he added a couple of cups of cold water from the bucket on the floor. He carried the almost empty teapot over to the sink and fished out half the old tea leaves. They felt cold and slimy against his fingers and he shook his hand over the sink to release them. He dried his hands on the back of his coat and retrieved the bag from the cupboard

and added another couple of pinches of dry leaves to the teapot. He folded the top of the bag and replaced it in the cupboard and carried the teapot back to the stove. He fished out his log book and wrote a note to himself on the back page, to remember to ask for an extra bag of tea in his next supplies.

He looked at the smoke unhurriedly unfurling itself from the head of the pipe.

He again thought of the dream.

He believed there was a certain complexity in the relationship between the raven and the people it was visiting, that went beyond the obvious messenger from the afterlife. It didn't make sense to him that Soule would dream that he had taken the form of a raven, merely to visit people to inform them of their upcoming demise.

He also believed Soule to be telling the truth, when he said that he didn't know why the dreams or visions were happening to him.

He checked his watch. Twelve minutes.

As he poured the now boiling water in the teapot, looking at the leaves swirling around in the hot liquid, he wondered if the black raven knew of the existence of the white raven and vice versa.

He poured a small amount of water in the cup and twirled it around a couple of times before pouring it back in the kettle. He replaced the kettle on the stove and picked up the two hot stones and slid them into his pockets. He then lifted the cup and the teapot off the stovetop, grabbed the lamp and made his way back upstairs.

He walked over to the table and carefully set down the pot and the cup. He removed his scarf and wrapped it around the teapot. As he made his way over to the window he checked his watch. Four minutes.

He scanned the horizon. Nothing moved.

He slowly and methodically wound the mechanism.

He made his way back to the table and sat down on the chair.

He flipped his coat collar and pulled it close, before reaching for the teapot to lightly swirl the contents.

He waited a while for the leaves to settle, before pouring tea into the cup. The steam spread like a hazy blanket over the surface, almost obscuring the amber liquid underneath.

He took a draw on the pipe and released a small cloud of smoke over the table, where it slowly intermingled with the steam.

He looked at the thinning pile of paper on the right.

He reached out and gently picked up a sheet.

The Actress

I was in a most peculiar space. It was a grayish white room that I can best define as round, although that is not an exact description. The ceiling was low and broken up into overlaying sections by irregular shaped tiles. A ridge, approximately a foot wide, was running the circumference of the room, between the wall and the ceiling. The ridge emitted a cold bright light through a multitude of narrow white opaque panels of glass.

The walls seemed to be made of a type of padded tiles, that were placed in a rather intricate pattern, from small to large or large to small.

Lining the walls were a series of strange looking openings, that looked like soft squares with their corners pushed in. Two of them were closed by grey metal shutters of peculiar design, the four others that were open appeared to lead into corridors or tunnels, that extended beyond what I could see from where I was situated. In the ceiling above my head a perfect circular opaque half globe was shining a plenary white light down onto a white tabletop that looked like it was made of flawless marble, although when I touched it, it didn't feel cold against my fingers. Above and around the light were a number of fixed devices inserted into the structure, each of them with a dark reflecting surface. They were not mirrors. They looked like photographs exhibited behind glass. A collection of glasses, plates and bowls were spread haphazardly on the tabletop, apparently with no regards to place setting or etiquette.

I was sitting on a circular bench of sorts made up by the joining of two chairs. The chairs were of an unusual design, made of thin white metal tubes with reddish brown cushions on the seat and the back. There was a set of chairs next to me and another two sets on the other side of the table.

A young woman was occupying one of the seats on the other side.

She was leaning back in the chair, reading a book. The long strong fingers of her right hand were spread out like a fan on the front cover.

Her left hand was absentmindedly playing with a curl of hair behind her ear. She was fair skinned and her dark curly hair was voluminous and unruly.

She had a high forehead and quite remarkable arched eyebrows over her large dark eyes. Her nose was straight and the lips of her rather small mouth were pressed together and slightly puckered, as if she was pondering a question.

She had a formidable jawline and strong symmetrical features. She was dressed in a mushroom brown jacket and a pair of loose fitting trousers. The jacket had a colourful half circle patch on either shoulder and looked like a uniform. It was unzipped and underneath I could see her white undershirt. It was snug against the contours of her slim body. The sleeves of her jacket were rolled up on her arms and one of her boot clad feet was *resting against the edge of the table.*

Although she appeared utterly at ease, she gave forth a pronounced confidence.

I realized I was staring at her and forced my eyes away and instead looked down at myself.

I was dressed in an identical mushroom coloured jacket and a somewhat loosely fitted cream cotton shirt, loose white trousers and white boots. I had similar multi coloured patches on each of my shoulders. When I lifted my arm I could read the word Nostromo arched over a picture of two green globes illuminated by a bright yellow star with a number underneath.

I thought it strange that the title of Conrad's novel was on the emblem.

My hands were pale, but large and strong and when I touched my face, I could feel a coarse beard, not dissimilar to my own, on my sturdy chin.

On the chair next to me lay what I first presumed to be an elongated black shiny helmet. However, when I took a closer look, I saw that it was the head of a most frightening creature. It was dark as Bakelite and had the appearance of a large beetle or some kind of dragon. It had a massive predatory mouth with rows upon rows of needle sharp teeth set in a sinewy jaw, under a wide curved head plate. I couldn't locate the creature's eyes, which strangely made it a lot more terrifying. Though I recognized that it couldn't possibly be alive, it was so horrid looking I was reminded of the devil himself.

Next to the head lay a pair of what looked like dismembered webbed hands, with tremendously long saber like claws at the end of dark skeletal fingers.

I felt extremely uncomfortable looking at this terrifying assembly, so I turned my head back to the woman instead.

She was looking over at me.

"Are you ok?" she asked. Her voice was husky and a lot deeper than I had expected. "You look like you have seen a ghost."

I lightly shook my head and rubbed at my temples with my fingers.

"I'm ok," I said. "What am I doing here?" My voice was deep and somewhat rugged sounding.

"Waiting." She looked at her bulky black wristwatch.

"One of the cameras quit and it's apparently going to take a couple of hours to replace it, so we're waiting. The others went to get something to eat, but I decided to stay here. It's not worth the trouble to go back to the trailer, and by the way you fell asleep and I didn't think it would be nice to leave you behind."

"Where are we?" I asked looking around.

"Are you sure you're ok?" she asked looking at me fixedly. "We're in the mess hall. We were about to shoot the chest-buster scene, when the camera quit." She paused. "Ridley was majorly disappointed because they'd just prepared John for the scene." She looked at me. "Don't you remember?"

"Of course," I said, "I'm just really tired."

"We're all tired." she said, reaching for one of the tall clear glasses on the table, "really fucking tired." She raised the glass and drank.

I was shocked by the indecency coming from her and it must have shown on my face, because she stopped her hand halfway to the table and looked at me questioningly.

"What's up with you?" she said. "Are you sure you're ok? You're certainly not your usual charming self."

"You can say that again," I replied, rubbing my forehead, looking at the book.

"What are you reading?" I asked after a while.

She leaned forward in her chair and held the book over the table for me to see. On the top half of the front of the book, there was a picture of the head of a white bird on a light creamy background. The bottom half of the book was charcoal gray and a formation of pointy rays were shooting out from the body of the bird. The inside of the bird's large dark eye was mesmerizing. It was as if the interior was occupied by a number of minuscule unchartered constellations in a self-contained autonomous firmament.

In between the stars the name Enoch was floating like a literal constellation. On a heavy grey separating line in the middle the title was written in black and yellow: The Somnambulist's Dreams.

She lifted her hand from the bottom of the book revealing the author's *name.*

"Are you familiar with his work?" she asked.

A cold sweat was rapidly forming on my forehead and I heard myself gasp in surprise.

When I recovered from my consternation, I quickly shook my head.

Oblivious to my obvious disquiet, the woman flipped through the pages rather casually.

"Neither am I. To be honest, I hadn't even heard of him before yesterday. Bo handed me this when I was bitching about re-reading Conrad. He said that I might enjoy it, and you know what? So far I do." She closed the book and looked at me.

"What is it about?" I asked, fearing the obvious answer.

"It's quite strange." she said and looked at me with her lips slightly pursed. "It's about the dreams, or visions I suppose, of a sleepwalking lighthouse keeper. So far, I've only read a handful of pages, so I can't really tell you too much about his dreams yet, but right now it's just nice to have something else to think about than Nostromo." She gestured at something to her left.

I couldn't see what she was pointing at, so I stood up and walked around the table. On the seat of one of the chairs lay a book. It had a light blue cloth cover with the title printed in gold letters on the front.

I picked it up and held it between my hands. It was Nostromo A Tale of the

Seaboard by Joseph Conrad.

"Are you reading this?" I asked the woman.

She looked at me with her large brown eyes as if I had said something amusing.

"You're joking right? We've all read it. Some of us several times. What's going on with you today, don't you remember anything? Ridley gave us all a copy, a couple of weeks before we started shooting. He wanted us all to understand the fundamentals of the storyline that apparently makes the name of this vessel so special." She pointed to the book I was holding. " Incidentally that's his private copy you're holding."

I didn't say anything, I just stood there staring at it.

"Are you sure you're ok? You seem different somehow, like you're not really here." She poked at my leg with her index finger.

"Yes, I'm ok," I answered, not knowing what else to say. "So are we making a movie of the book?"

She looked up at me and threw her head back and laughed. She had a wonderfully free and vacillating laugh, that reverberated in the space.

"You're seriously out of whack today," she said smiling. "Have you hit your head on something? She looked at me again and stopped laughing. "Do you really not know what's going on?"

"I'm not entirely sure," I said. "Somehow my presence here feels familiar, and yet I cannot seem to recall what I am supposed to do."

"You sound different." She looked at me searchingly.

"I do? I wasn't aware of that."

"You really do. It's like you're using a different vocabulary. Like somebody else is talking, using your voice." She looked at me questioningly. "You're not getting sick are you?"

"No," I replied. "I'm not sick."

"Then what is it?" She smiled at me with her head slightly tilted.

"I don't know," I said, not wanting to upset her, "I feel somewhat displaced, I suppose."

She smiled up at me. "Perhaps you just need to do something else to take your mind off things."

She got up from her chair and took my hand in hers. Although a bit smaller than my own, her hand was warm and strong.

She turned around and led me through one of the openings in the wall.

"Where are we going?" I asked, looking around.

"Where we always go, when we want to take our minds off things." She squeezed my hand.

We were in an octagonal corridor.

It was quite a claustrophobic space. There were a large amount of grey pipes running along the walls and some of the wall panels looked like they belonged in the engine room of a ship.

However, nothing was moving. It didn't smell of oil or coal either, and it wasn't noisy. In fact, our footsteps on the iron-grid on the floor were the only sounds in the space.

We walked around a corner and almost knocked over a large camera on a tripod, standing in the center of the corridor.

She stopped and carefully walked around the camera, then she turned right and lead me into a most extraordinary space.

We were in a creamy white octagonal room, approximately ten by ten feet across.

At first glance it looked like a small chapel.

On the floor a raised brown platform about a foot high and two feet wide was circling the room and a large white padded chair was standing in the center.

The ceiling was bisected by an equidistant cross and four rhombus shaped skylights, that were emitting a soft white light through opaque panels.

Most unusual though, were the thousands of small white lights inserted in the walls and the ceiling. They were behind opaque square panes of glass, blinking on and off in in a disharmonious pattern.

Embedded in the center of the sectioned walls every couple of feet was a glass covered frame. Matching the frames in the mess hall, these were also empty and only reflected what was already in the space.

The woman walked over to the chair. She stood in front of me, put her hands on my chest and gently pushed me into the seat.

I didn't know what to expect, but I was completely taken aback when she began removing her jacket. I was astounded by her boldness and lack of reserve and even more so when she loosened her belt and unzipped her trousers, that now liberated fell to the floor and came to rest around her ankles.

She was effectively undressed, bar the smallest white undergarments and her snug fitting undershirt.

She stood in front of me, with her hands on her hips, looking at me expectantly.

Although I realized that I was a participant in a regular activity, I didn't know how to react, so I just kept gazing at her almost nude body.

She was beautiful standing there surrounded by the lights and I realized that I wanted her.

She didn't utter a word as she leaned down and pulled at the sleeves of my jacket. I lifted my arms to assist her.

On the inside of my left arm there was a large tattoo of a black raven sitting on the head of a bust of a woman wearing an ornate helmet.

I had the strangest feeling that the raven was purposely staring at me with its icy blue eye.

When she had removed my jacket, she unbuttoned my shirt and slid her hands underneath it.

They felt charged against my skin.

She pulled my cream shirt and light green undershirt over my head and threw them on the floor. Her hands moved to my belt. She expertly unbuckled it and pulled me up by my hands. When I was standing, she slowly pulled down my trousers and undergarment.

I was now completely naked and could not hide the rigid state of my organ. She was not affectedly shy by my condition, on the contrary, she looked at me and smiled.

She slid her own undergarments down her legs and dropped them on the floor.

I could feel the heat of her body as she moved closer to me.

She emitted a subtle yet enticing infused smell of perspiration, lilies and sandalwood.

She pushed me back in the chair, lifted her left leg and straddled me.

She looked intently into my eyes and used her left hand to guide me inside her.

She unhurriedly pushed herself down until our pubic bones met.

She pulled her undershirt over her head, dropped it on the floor and reached for my hands. She locked my hands in hers over my head on the back of the chair and began to move her hips slowly up and down. •

She kept her eyes on mine as she undulated.

Her pupils were dilated and piceous like the bottom of an amaranthine well.

I looked into her eyes.

I was convinced I saw something, like a speck of light, move in their depth.

She was slowly increasing her speed on my lap and her breathing intensified. She dug her fingers into the back of my hands and pressed them hard against the headrest of the chair.

She was still looking at me intensely and moved her head a little closer to mine while lithely moving her body.

There was unmistakably something moving deep inside her. It looked like a tiny snowflake carelessly drifting in the wind. I tried to focus on the movement of the flake as her breathing deepened and she opened her mouth gasping for air.

She began to shake as if a small electric current was running through her. Her insides contracted and squeezed around my organ.

I looked into the bottomless well and from the depth of the darkness the shape began to take form.

It was a white raven flying towards the light.

I thought I could hear it calling.

As it reached the surface, I ruptured into a million little pieces.

When I regained my senses, I was sitting in a chair in the watch room. The rays of the sun were blindingly streaming through the windows and it was warm in the room. My upper body was bare and my breeches were in a pile around my ankles on the floor. My hands were holding on to the chair behind my head and I could feel a pressure on my upper legs. I looked down and saw a sack of flour lying on my lap.

Although I ultimately accept this as a dream, I must admit that I am terribly embarrassed by my conduct. Still, I made the promise to be as faithful in my description as I possibly can. As I have stated many times before, I am without control in my somnambular state and therefore cannot be responsible for my actions, however deplorable.

Though my actions perhaps speak otherwise, I can assure you that I have no romantic feelings towards the woman in the dream. You should know that you are the only true love of my life and that I have never laid desirous eyes on another woman. I ask once again that you not be abhorred by the fantasies of my mind and that you judge me purely for who I am as a husband to you and as a father to our girls.

I cannot explain the dream any better than you. I have no possible explanation for why I was there.

It does not seem that these events have a logical design or a specific purpose, and I find it increasingly difficult to connect the recurring elements.

Although I recognize it is all an absurd elaborate fantasy made by my overzealous mind, I am nonetheless haunted by the devilish head and claws.

I believe I am perfectly lucid in my cognizant state, yet my mind is not at ease.

He put the sheet down on top of the pile on the left.

He sat quietly with his hands folded in his lap and gazed into the distance. His fingers were cold so he put his hands in his pockets to feel for the stones.

They were barely warm.

He un-pocketed his watch and checked the time. Twenty eight minutes.

He stood up and walked to the window. It was still about four hours to sunrise and yet the night sky had already altered its complexion. For a while he looked at the constellations in the expanse above, then he moved his eyes down to scan the horizon. On the surface the sea seemed as calm as the sky.

He walked over to the bucket on the floor and unbuttoned his jacket. He held the jacket aside as he unbuckled his trousers and took out his member. He had to wait until his erection subsided before he could let go of his water. He stood for a while staring at the etching of the bird on the branch on the wall in front of him, trying not to think of anything.

When he was finally able to let go, he watched the fuliginous stream of urine splash onto the surface of the liquid already amassed in the bucket. It left a trace of musty, salty odor in the air.

He finished, tucked himself away and went back to the table to pick up the cup, teapot and lamp. He walked downstairs to the galley, where he deposited the teapot on the end of the stove, put the cup in the sink and washed his hands.

He withdrew the two cold stones from his pockets and placed them on the stovetop next to the others.

He put the kettle on the stove and walked over to the pantry and grabbed a small package of oats from the shelf.

He walked back to the sink and picked up the pan. There was dried residue from the beans congealed on the inside, so he poured some warm water from the kettle into the pan. After he rinsed it he put the clean pan on the stove, picked up the cup and measured out a cup of oats and dropped them in the pan. He then added a cup and a half of cold water and walked over to the cupboard and took a pinch of salt from the jar and tossed it in the pan.

He checked his watch. Sixteen minutes.

As he waited for the porridge to heat up, he thought about the latest vision.

Although he didn't regard himself as a profligate, he wasn't exactly a saint either and couldn't evade the fact that he had been aroused by Soule's narration.

The description of the encounter with the woman was especially expressive and even though Soule had claimed the event to be a dream, he thought the account read more like a confession. It was clear from the description that Soule himself believed that he had made love to the woman, or rather that the woman had made love to him.

It was his belief that Soule genuinely believed a metamorphosis was taking place and that, rather than dreaming, he was being disestablished into an alternative story, perhaps even in a different era. It was obvious to him that Soule was confounded by the apocryphal images and events, yet he continued to write about the accounts in a composed and rational manner. He didn't know what to make of the narrative.

It was evident that Soule had visited an actress on a movie set and that it somehow had a connection to Conrad's novel, but he couldn't think of any correlations that made sense. Also, the woman had laughed when Soule had asked her if they were making a movie of the book, so he was uncertain of its implication.

He very much appreciated Conrad's novel and had always had an affinity for old Giorgio, even when he made the ultimate mistake at the end. He thought about the setting of the novel, its revolutionary narrative and the development of the main character, but he simply couldn't connect it to anything Soule had described.

The rooms he had visited and the other images all sounded alien to him.

He walked over to the sink cabinet and picked up a wooden spoon from the drawer.

He wondered if the head of the devilish creature was purely allegorical. It reminded him of Nosferatu and the creatures of hell in Hieronymus Bosch's paintings and he was curious if it had a tangible function. Maybe it was part of a totem or a gargoyle, or perhaps another actor would wear it as a mask like a golem to frighten the woman. It was conceivable that they had been filming a horror movie, but if that was the case, he couldn't establish a logical connection to Conrad.

He stuck the spoon in the pan and stirred the content. The ingredients had not yet condensed, but the semi opaque water was simmering on the surface, so he knew that it wouldn't be long before it thickened. He kept stirring the gray bubbling mass around the pan until it reached a gelatinous consistency. When it was to his liking, he removed the pan from the stovetop and used the wooden spoon as a ladle and scooped the steaming porridge into the bowl. He put the pan back in the sink and grabbed the bag of sugar from the top shelf in the pantry.

He sprinkled a generous amount onto the porridge and put the bag back in the cupboard. He checked the time. Six minutes. He picked up two of the hot stones and slipped them into his pockets.

He stuck a spoon in the porridge, picked up the bowl and made his way back upstairs.

He deposited the bowl of steaming porridge on the table and walked over to rewind the mechanism.

He counted the revolutions and when he was certain the weights were all the way up, he walked back to the table, sat down on the chair and picked up the bowl and put it in the palm of his hand.

The steam was warming his face as he leant over the table to pick up another sheet of paper.

He placed it on the tabletop in front of him.

The Taxidermist

I was in a large room. The walls were the colour of ash and the white ceiling, high above, was dirty with large patches of paint peeling off, clinging to its host like a layer of discarded reptilian skin.

Sunlight was streaming through the blinds of three dominant windows and the semi obfuscated light cast a collinear pattern on the floor near where I was sitting.

I looked down and saw a pair of reddish scaly legs ending in a set of pink claws. They were imbedded on the white shoulder bump of what I assumed to be an animal of the bovine family. It had small curvy horns and was lying down on a patch of sandy dirt in a rather sizable raised frame on the floor.

There was a penetrating mephitic smell in the dusty air, like a mixture of dried meat, burnt almonds and formaldehyde.

I jumped around on the animal's back.

There was no movements under the skin and it didn't release any heat either. On the wall opposite, the giant head of a water buffalo was blindly staring at my antics, and I belatedly realized that I was perched on top of a stuffed bull.

I flapped my ivory wings and released a considerable amount of dust that drifted into the air. The particles created a ductile pattern in the beams of sunlight.

I looked around.

The room was overflowing with articles that one would usually find in a museum of natural history or in the studio of a taxidermist.

There were a number of African specimens in the room.

At the opposite end of the studio, a large gorilla was standing on its feet, in front of a large amount of stacked hay bales. It was pouting and locked in the pose of mutely drumming its chest with its muscular arms. Next to the gorilla stood an enormous grey rhinoceros with its massive horned head in the air. It was placed on a low sand filled pedestal on the ground and one of its trunk like front legs was bent as if the animal was ready to charge. A small group birds were clustered on the rhino's back. They were, more or less, the size of a common sparrow and brownish green in colour with vivid red beaks.

Closer to where I was sitting, a male lion with a lavish dark mane was standing on a smaller rectangular platform next to a lioness.

She was lying on the sandy ground with her front paws crossed, vacuously gazing into the distance. The male lion was silently roaring and its huge canine teeth looked nearly white against its pink nudibranch-like tongue.

In one of the corners, four rolls of wire, differing in thickness, were leaning against the wall next to a bundle of thin steel rods lying on the floor.

A sizable metal framed table with a grey stone top stood in the center of the room. Brushes, wires and an assortment of small hand tools lay scattered on its surface. A large plasmic shape, made from hay and twine, was sitting in the middle of the table and the front part of a zebra hide was hanging over the edge.

Even in this environment the zebra's flattened contours and abandoned arrangement appeared incongruous.

There were a couple of birds placed in sand filled frames on the ground.

One of them I recognized as a guinea fowl, but the other one I hadn't seen before. It was some type of Ibis. Its body was white, but its neck, downwards curved beak, long legs and rump feathers were all black as velvet. The head was turned and its neck was bent downwards, as if it was looking for something on the ground.

In one of the corners, near a massive sliding grey metal door, stood a large glass cabinet. The three shelves near the top were filled with an assemblage of specimen jars and the lower two shelves with a multitude of dark glass bottles and metal cans.

From where I was sitting, it looked like there was a great variety of smaller mammals and snakes in the jars.

There were also several quite ordinary wooden pedestals in the room. A couple were empty, but most of them displayed a smallish grey sculpture of an animal.

An older man stood by the pedestal closest to me.

In all aspects he was quite ordinary looking. He was medium built with slightly arcuated shoulders.

His head was of normal size and his thinning grey hair was carefully combed over his balding crown. It glistened in the sunlight.

His face was neither elongated nor round and his small pointy ears lay flat against his head.

His deep-set bluish grey eyes sat somewhat close together under his unruly brow, and the salient bags underneath were puffy and perse.

His straight, not too protruding nose, sat central over a smallish mouth, that was pulled down on one side by a curved dark wood pipe.

Two distinct furrows were running down either side of his face, from the side of his nose to the small jowls by his sturdy chin.

He was wearing a white shirt and a thin black tie, stuck into his shirt between two buttons, to keep it out of the way. His shirt sleeves were rolled up over his elbows and his forearms looked fibrous and strong.

His dusty clay covered hands were wide and the fingers short but slim.

His brown tweed trousers sat high on his waist and were held in place by a thin black belt with a brass buckle. His dark brown leather shoes were in dire need of a polish and one of the shoelaces had come undone and was flattened on the floor like a dried up night-crawler on the sidewalk.

The man was working on an animal and his hands were in continuous motion, either adding or subtracting clay to or from the surface.

After a while he stopped working and took a couple of steps back.

He walked around the pedestal and slowly turned his head from side to side to survey his work.

It was a small sculpture of a water buffalo being attacked by a big cat. The buffalo's tail was raised in alarm. The front of its body was turned and its head with its potent horns was low to the ground to fend off the big cat crouching by its flanks, ready to pounce.

It was an exquisite pose. Not only did it demonstrate the pure muscular power and dynamism of both animals, but it superbly conveyed the raw brutality of life.

"Not bad, not bad at all," the man said to himself. His voice was higher than I expected and rather nasal. "What do you think?" he said and turned around to face me. "Not bad, eh?" He pushed out his lower lip when he talked. It sounded a bit like he chewed his words on their way out.

"What?" I said, baffled that he didn't seem at all surprised by my presence. "Not bad, I said." he replied removing his pipe.

"No," I said, "not bad at all. I admit that I am not familiar with the world of animal portraiture, but this is clearly incredible work."

"Thank you," he said, "that's high praise indeed. Although I do believe I still have a bit to do on the reflex action on the lower part of the left hind leg by the insertion of the calf muscle. There's something about it that isn't quite right." He pointed to a spot on the leg with the end of his pipe, which

obscured my view. "However, I better give it a rest for a while. I find it often helps if I come back to a problem with fresh eyes."

He picked up a small glass spray bottle from the base of the pedestal, walked around the sculpture and intermittently pressed a rubber bulb to release a fine mist, that fell like a watery haze on the clay. He rubbed his hands on a large dirtied cotton cloth, that he gently placed over the piece and sprayed with water.

He replaced the spray bottle on the floor and walked over to sit down on one end of an elegantly shaped mahogany couch, that stood in front of the middle window.

He leaned against the pink floral back, stretched his legs and kicked off his shoes. He let out a satisfying sigh as he wiggled his black socked toes in the air.

"That's better," he said, with his right hand rummaging his shirt pocket. It came up with a flat white package of matches that he put on the frayed upholstery beside him. He leant forward and picked up a small narrow red can of tobacco from the three legged, round mahogany coffee table. He casually emptied the content of his pipe into a large tin ashtray that sat in the center of the table, by dabbing the head of the pipe against the palm of his hand. It made a hollow popping sound when it connected.

When he was satisfied the pipe was empty, he began stuffing it with fresh tobacco.

He looked at me from across the room.

*"To what do I owe the pleasure?" he asked, putting the can back on the
table and opening the match book.*

*He removed a match, lit it and moved the flame slowly over the pipe bowl.
The flame disappeared between the strands of tobacco in harmony with his
inhalation and appeared reborn with his exhalation. After a few puffs, the
tobacco in the top of the pipe began to glow and he blew out a cloud of
smoke, that swirled like a phantom in the air above him and spread a nutty
sweet aroma in the room.*

He waved his hand to extinguish the match and dropped it in the ashtray.

"Well?" he said.

*"I really don't know? I wasn't planning this in advance," I answered,
totally caught off guard by the ease with which he accepted my appearance.*

*"No, I am aware of that," he said looking amused. I thought I could see his
eyes twinkling through the brume.*

*"You are not the first interlocutor in my studio you know." He pointed to
the wall behind me, on which a square beveled edged oak mount was placed
about seven feet off the ground. The mount was about a foot and a half
wide and a couple of inches deep and a stripped knurled oak branch was
protruding about a foot horizontally into the air. A couple of inches below
the branch a small rectangular brass plaque had been inserted into the
wood.*

The mount was empty.

From where I was sitting, I couldn't read the text on the plaque, so I spread my wings and flew up. I landed on the branch and bent down to read the text on the plaque.

Corvus Corax (Albus) it said.

"What do you think?" he said. "I had it made after your last visit. Given the circumstances, I thought it was quite the appropriate solution.

If somebody comes knocking, you just fly up there and sit still for a while. Just choose your position with care, so you don't have to struggle keeping it. Something simple will do." He smiled and raised his free hand to wave me over.

I flew to where he was sitting and landed on the arm of the couch. The lacquered surface was smooth and slippery and I found it difficult to keep my balance, so I jumped down and sat on the couch instead.

"I have been here before?" I said. "That's strange, I don't remember that."

"No, but you've been here quite a few times actually." He waved at the smoke with his hand. "But why you come here is still a mystery. I originally thought that your appearance here was no different than the other apparitions, but when you began talking to me, I realized something out of the ordinary was happening."

He turned his head to look at me.

"What do you mean by the other apparitions?" I asked, searching the room

for anything unusual. "Wouldn't you say that seeing ghosts is out of the ordinary?"

"Perhaps your ordinary is different from my ordinary. In my experience, what is real are the things that are still there, even after you stop believing in them."

He took a drag on his pipe and released another cloud of smoke into the air. "Besides, I shouldn't have used the word apparition. Visitant is probably more descriptive."

"But isn't that technically the same as an apparition?" I asked.

"Perhaps it is to you," he replied, "but to me it is not." His tone wasn't demonstrative or aggressive. He merely stated the facts.

"So what do they do, these visitants?" I asked. "Are they here now?" I again looked around the room for evidence of the occult. Finding none, I looked back at the man.

He smiled at me and shook his head.

"No," he said, "there's nobody there right now. They're sometimes here, when I work at bringing their bodies back, but only sometimes. It's not like they're hovering in the air above me either. Occasionally they just appear next to their physical form." He removed the pipe from his mouth, leant forward in his seat and looked at his socked feet.

"As a rule they don't seem interested in communicating with me. For the most part they just stand on the floor looking at themselves, or should I say;

look at what they used to be. This is especially true for the larger mammals. They also seem to linger for extended periods of time, but maybe that's only because it takes a lot longer for me to bring them back."

He leaned back in his seat.

"Although now and again, when I am close to finishing a job, some walk in and out of their physical manifest, as if they're trying to fuse with their old self."

He slowly shook his head and ran his hand across his chin.

"It's a disparaging sight when the agglutination fails, and they move back and forth in their old form to get their contours to align." He puffed on his pipe and looked at the drifting smoke in the sunlight.

"When they finally realize they can't return to their physical form, most of them just disappear. However, others return from time to time, and whenever they do, their presence noticeably weakens, until I can barely see them at all."

He looked around and gestured to the room at large.

"Perhaps I was wrong in saying that there's nobody there."

I looked at the conglomeration of dust particles dancing in the sun filled air and wondered if they were indeed ghostly remnants of the animals in the room.

"You know there's really nothing there, when you look at them," he said after a while.

He looked around from animal to animal.

"They're essentially an assembly of objects, that happen to carry the characteristics of something living. However, most of us refuse to accept it."

He paused and looked at the mounted water buffalo on the wall.

"Even in these animals' eternal stasis, our mind urges them to be alive, because, without the utter destruction or removal of the physical body, we cannot possibly comprehend the concept of death. As long as there is a viable physical presence, we rebut death as a feasible option and cling to the hope of miraculous reanimation. We of course have the resurrection and the adherent believers to blame for this."

He took a long drag on his pipe and without removing it, he let out a cloud of smoke from the side of his mouth.

"But are your visitants not in some way resurrected?" I asked, ruffling my back feathers. "They do come back from the dead, do they not?"

"If you believe that I liken my creations to the effigy of Christ, you are mistaken," he said earnestly. "Coming back from the dead is an improbability. When the shadow of an animal visits, it is in no way coming back from the dead. Although it might be attempting to reconnect with its physical form, it's still very much in a different realm."

He looked at me intensely.

"Perhaps, because I am the only one who can see them, they're real only to

me." He paused and looked at the white bull on the floor. Its ears were pointing downwards and its brown eyes were purposelessly gazing at the sandy ground.

"Do you find my words to be at odds with my profession?" he asked, but continued before I had a chance to respond.

"If you do, I can assure you that I don't think my philosophy in any way interferes with my job. Rather, I believe it generally enhances my work, as I am basically trying to create the most believable scenario for the viewer. I want the viewer to think that whatever object they're looking at, potentially could snarl, roar or charge at them, although I am completely aware of the futility involved in the exercise."

He looked at me through the smoke.

"No," I said, " I don't believe there's anything wrong in wanting to make a display that is as realistic as possible." I stretched one of my wings down over the edge of the couch.

"However, it's not about realism," he replied. "It's much closer to a circus act. Even though our rational mind tells us it's not possible for an elephant to vanish into thin air, our subconscious mind desperately entreats the elephant to do so. And when it does, we're not asking pertinent questions about placement of mirrors, lighting or props. We just revel in the fact that the animal is no longer visible."

He turned his head and looked at me.

"Do you understand what I am saying?"

"I believe so," I replied.

"Death becomes a substitute for life," he said unpretentiously, looking down at his hands that lay folded in his lap. "We eradicate the real and replace it, thousands of miles away, with a Lilliputian illusion. Nothing you see is real. In many ways, asking you to believe any of this as a representation of reality, it's no different than asking you to follow the rabbit down the rabbit hole."

He again gestured with his hand to the objects in the room.

"You know what my wife calls me?" He paused and looked at me. "She calls me the zoologist's Dr. Frankenstein."

As he smiled a collection of fine lines, like river beds in a dry landscape, appeared in the corner of his eyes.

"Her voice is always quite playful, but underneath I detect a lick of truth. She knows that there's nothing I would rather do, than bring them all back to life."

He ran his hand across his forehead and patted down a couple of strands of loose hairs on the top of his scalp.

"However, as that is an improbability, all that is left for me to do, is a feeble attempt to respectfully recondition the unequalled beauty of these creatures and in doing so, mourn their passing." He drew on his pipe and let out another cloud of smoke.

"That sounds suspiciously antithetical to me," I said. "Didn't you say earlier that your work had nothing to do with resurrection?" I jumped around on the couch to face him. "Yet it sounds very much to me like you're attempting to reanimate the dead."

"I don't believe I used the word resurrection," he said solemnly. "But no matter what I said, I am afraid there's no escaping my eternal impasse: The futility of breathing cursory life into something undeniably dead."

He shook his head and looked up at me. There were tears in his eyes.

"I am forever deadlocked," his voice intermingled with the smoke dissipating in the sunlight.

For a while neither of us spoke.

We were quietly looking at the drifting particles and swirling bands of smoke emitting from the pipe.

"Why do you continue to come here?" he asked, turning to face me. "When you first visited, I believed your visit was a forewarning or an omen of some kind? Now, I'm not so sure what to believe. If you're not an emissary or harbinger, why do you come here?"

"I honestly don't know," I said. "I don't even know how I get here."

I hopped up on the table, flapped my wings and accidently knocked over the tobacco can. It made a dull metallic sound as it fell.

As he reached for the can to stand it back up, I heard footsteps outside the door.

He had clearly heard them too.

He looked at me meaningfully and made a small movement with his head. I followed his eyes to the empty mount on the wall.

I took flight and landed on the branch. I sat completely still and looked towards the door.

The light from the doorway obliterated the striations from the window blinds, as it swept across the floor.

"......and this is where he used to do the majority of his work."

It was the voice of a young man I heard, as the elements in the room dissolved.

The light permeated the space and I found myself adrift.

I awoke sitting on the table in the watch room.

I was in the nude, but for a white bed sheet wrapped around my shoulders and hanging down by my arms. My legs were tucked together under my body and my toes were clutching at the edge of the table. The sunlight was blinding and as I opened my eyes it took a while before I could bring my surroundings into focus.

The smell of tobacco was hanging in the air and when I looked down, I saw my pipe lying on its side next to me on the table. It was emanating a faint wispy spiral of smoke. I almost fell off the table in my attempt to get down. My legs were bereft of life and it took me a considerable amount of time to get the blood circulating again.

Although It is impossible for me to fully understand these dreams, I realize that my latest dream is somehow connected to the other dreams. I thought I recognized the white bull on the floor from an earlier dream, but why it was there, I do not know. In fact I don't even know if it was the same bull or just a bizarre coincidence.

Although I know it goes against everything I have described in this recent recollection, I have the strongest suspicion that the taxidermist was not really there when I visited, but that he himself was nothing but an aberration. I can't comprehend why I would encounter him as phantasm in my dream. What is the reason that I did not visit him when he was still alive? Or was he alive when I visited him before, as he claimed I had?

Alas, I have no answers to the questions I am asking myself.

I promise you, that what I am recounting is a truthful account of the events. I am writing everything down as I recall it and though it is difficult to remember the exact details, I do try not to leave anything out.

He put the piece of paper down on the growing pile on the left.

His hands were freezing and he could hardly feel himself releasing the sheet.

He put his hands in his pockets to search for the stones. When he found them, they were equally cold to the touch. He took off his gloves, brought his hands to his mouth and blew into the hollow he created between them. When he could feel the warm moist air in the palm of his hands, he rubbed them against each other until his fingers began prickling. He pulled his jacket together, wrapped the scarf around his neck and got up from the chair.

He walked over to the window.

The light had changed considerably during the last hour. The darkness was less impenetrable and the stars in the sky had lost some of their candescence.

On the horizon the sky was an almost translucent sapphire blue.

He could just about make out a faint hint of copper against the darker surface of the sea.

Another dawn was approaching.

He checked his watch. Twenty two minutes.

He went back to the table to pick up the bowl and lamp.

He walked downstairs to the galley, where he deposited the bowl and spoon in the sink and placed the lamp on the edge of the stove.

He grabbed the kettle, removed the lid and poured a couple of cups of water from the bucket inside. He replaced the lid and put the kettle back on the stove. He dug out the stones from his pockets and placed them on the stovetop next to the other two.

He fetched the teapot, poured the cold tea into the sink and removed most of the old leaves before placing the teapot on the end of the stove next to the stones.

He thought about Soule's dream.

There was no question in his mind that the white bull was the same as the one from the first dream. He had even flipped back through the pages to reread the description.

He wondered how the bull had ended up on the floor in the taxidermist studio and how long it had been there.

The taxidermist had obviously died some time before Soule's visit.

However, considering the amount of work on display in his studio, he couldn't have been dead long.

Although, there was always the possibility that the studio was used as storage space. That would certainly explain the amount of animals on display.

He also wondered if the taxidermist knew that he was a

phantasm or whether he believed himself to be alive.

Judging from Soule's account, it seemed as if the taxidermist had no idea that he was in a different realm. During his conversation with Soule, he had given no indications at all that he believed himself to be dead. As a matter of fact, right up to the point where the door opened, it had seemed like he was very much alive.

He checked his watch. Fourteen minutes.

He walked over to fetch the bag of tea leaves from the cupboard. "Damn it."

He had dropped the bag on the floor. A small amount of tea spilled out forming a small brown fanlike pattern against the grey background.

He bent down to scoop at the leaves with his hand.

He picked up the loose leaves off the floor and dumped them in the teapot, closed the bag and put it back on the shelf.

It seemed obvious from the dreams that Soule was somehow bestowed a role as either messenger or recipient and that the dreams were often occurring in the vicinity of death. But now, when he thought about it, he couldn't really be sure that was indeed the case.

While it was true that the first couple of dreams had doubtlessly involved death as a crucial element in the narrative, most of the dreams had not.

Perhaps it was fair to say that death, although central to all things in life, was merely a peripheral ingredient in majority of the visions and that he had put too much emphasis on the fact that the black raven was a symbolic harbinger of death and that he therefore had positioned the white raven as a messenger of life.

However, he couldn't be sure that the roles to which he had unintentionally consigned the ravens, were in truth accurate. Though he found it difficult to think of anything offhand, it was still conceivable that the meaning behind their colouration could be something else entirely.

He picked up the kettle and poured the boiling water into the teapot and a little in the cup. He placed the kettle on the end of the stove and picked up the two hot stones and slipped them into his pockets.

He grabbed the cup, teapot and lamp and walked back upstairs. He deposited the items on the table and walked over to the window.

Everything was quiet.

A faint whitish golden band was shimmering above the horizon, dividing the sea and the sky into two separate elements. He knew it wouldn't be long before the rays of the sun would break the liquid palisade and brighten the infinite expanse once again. He often wondered what might someday be discovered out there beyond what could be observed.

Endlessness perhaps.

He checked the time.

Four minutes.

He walked over to the mechanism and began the last rewind of the night.

He counted the revolutions and felt for the point of tension.

When he was assured of the weights' position, he stopped and walked back to the table. He pulled out the chair and sat down.

He lifted the teapot of the table and moved it in small circular motions to agitate the leaves. After a while he put the teapot back on the table, waited a bit and slowly poured some of the tea into the cup.

He then unrolled his scarf and wrapped it around the teapot.

He pulled his jacket tight against his neck and fished out his pipe from his pocket and smacked the opening against the palm of his hand. Small lumps of blackened tobacco mixed with ashes fell to the floor by his feet.

He ran his boot over them, leaving a grey and black smeared

striation behind.

As he stuffed his pipe with fresh tobacco, he looked at the diminished pile on the right. Gauging from the thinness of the pile, he reckoned that Soule's dreams were coming to an end.

He rummaged in his pockets and found the book of matches.

When he enkindled the tobacco, he generated a substantial cloud of smoke around him.

He looked at the swirling haze drifting in

the air and breathed in the luscious aroma.

He stuck the pouch back in his pocket and reached out to pick up another sheet of paper from the pile.

The Cell

The room was probably no more than six by eight feet and everything in it was a feculent shade of white.

The heavy steel door, with a small hatch at eye height and a narrow low hatch close to the floor, had no handle and the small rectangular window opposite was barred and had a substantial wire mesh placed in front of the thick glass.

The pane of glass on the low right hand side was missing and I could feel the cold air on my face as it the blew unhindered into the room.

Gauging from the colour of the sky and the light coming through the window, it was either early in the morning or late in the afternoon.

I was sitting on a white metal stool next to narrow rectangular white metal table. Across from me a metal bed frame, with an insufficient grimy looking mattress and an almost diaphanous wool blanket, was pushed up against the wall.

The table and the bed were bolted to the grey stone floor.

I was wearing a rough-hewn white shirt and a pair of oversized trousers that was fastened at my waist with a large button.

My feet were covered by a pair of mottled grey woolen socks, that had been darned so many times, it was difficult to tell if any part of them was still the original wool.

At first glance my hands looked like my own and when I ran my fingers

over the contours of my face and through my hair everything seemed

familiar. My beard was perhaps a little longer than usual and my hair

somewhat unruly, but otherwise It seemed like I was indeed inhabiting my

own body.

I looked around the room.

Above me the dirtied ceiling was peeling and the paint had been forcibly

removed from the furniture to such a degree that their surfaces looked

mosaic.

The walls had been painted numerous times, yet the paint couldn't hide the

myriad of declarations that had been clawed or scraped into the surface.

Except from the sparse furnishings, there was very little else in the room.

In the corner behind the table, a steel bucket, with a severely dented flat lid,

emitted a foul smell. A couple of sheets of paper lay in a small pile on the

tabletop next to a small inkwell, a blotter and a much used quill with a

flayed tip.

I picked up one of the sheets. The paper was of reasonably good quality.

I held it up against the fading light. It was white with no distinguishing

marks and all the sheets were blank.

I looked back at the walls.

From the ground to about two feet from the ceiling, the walls exhibited a

phenomenal amount of scribbles, drawings and other proclamations. They were like a multilayered tapestry that, except where it was interrupted by the window, ran the circumference of the room.

The inscriptions varied in scale, depth and eloquence and had obviously been produced over a considerable amount of time. Not even the heavy metal door had been immune to the graphic onslaught and had had quite a few obscenities haphazardly scratched into both its frame and surface.

I got up from the stool, took two small steps forward and leant down to run my hand over the wall above the bed, where the inscriptions were most prevalent.

Besides the many obscenities, both written and clearly delineated in drawings, one of the more intelligible inscriptions caught my eye.

Although small, the lettering was concise and rather elegant. It looked like it could have been scraped into the wall with a needle or a very thin nail and the person who wrote it had obviously endeavoured to arrange the sentences so that they aligned.

Dying is to be regarded as the real aim of life
The moment we die everything is decided
All else is but a futile exercise

I reckoned from the lack of paint that the text had been inscribed fairly recently and I looked around the room to see if I could find another example of the handwriting.

After searching a while through the expressive morass, I located another

text in the same hand high above the table.

nothing ever comes into being

or ceases to be

I stepped off the table and sat down on the stool.

Both inscriptions seemed familiar and I was convinced I had either heard or

read them somewhere quite recent.

However, no matter how hard I ransacked my brain, I could not recall

where that might have been.

The harder I tried to remember, the more elusive it became.

Instead I walked over to the window to look out.

The disappearing light indicated that it was nearing evening. A dense fog

was obscuring my view and I couldn't see much of the surrounding

landscape. A wide winding graveled path leading away from the building

cut through the long grass, and in the middle distance a group of tall

cypresses were breaking through the fog.

In the developing darkness, they looked like finger tips reaching up from

under a surface, desperately searching for a stronghold.

I walked back and sat on the bed. I could feel the cold hard metal on my buttocks through the meager fabric of the mattress.

I wondered what I was doing in this cell. Had I been imprisoned for committing a crime? Judging from the austere surroundings and the lack of company, the crime must have been serious. Was I a murderer? If so, who's life had I taken?

Or could it be that this wasn't a prison at all, but some kind of sanatorium? If that held true, why was I here?

I stood up and walked over to the door.

I ran my finger on the inside of the small hatch, before kneeling down to examine the second hatch that was positioned low to the ground. It was narrow and wide.

I guessed that was where the food tray would appear. I was curious when I was going to get fed and who was bringing the food.

I got up and walked back to the stool and sat down.

The room was soundless.

All I could hear was my own breathing and the unreasonably loud screeching of the legs of the metal stool scraping against the stone floor. I pressed my ear against the wall. I heard nothing but the sound of rushing blood.

I sat back down on the stool, picked up one of the sheets of paper, placed it on the table in front of me and reached for the quill. I turned the quill between my fingers and opened the inkwell. I thought about dipping the quill but the light was rapidly fading, draining the colour from the already anemic room.

Instead I replaced the quill and got up from the stool.

I rubbed the side of my neck as I walked back to the window and looked into the approaching night.

By now the fog had enveloped almost everything and it was difficult to distinguish anything other than the grey floating mass.

I stood by the window, looking into the swirling mist, when I heard a metallic clang behind me. I turned around and saw a tray had been pushed through the low hatch.

I walked over to the door, picked up the tray and carried it the short distance to the table, where I put it down.

Besides a bowl of drab gruel and a cup of water there were a number of unexpected items on the tray. A white wax candle was lying next to a box of matches and a small, already stuffed, pipe.

I picked up the pipe and sniffed at the tobacco. The scent was sweet and aromatic. I thought it was familiar, but no matter how hard I tried, I couldn't recall where I had encountered it before.

I put the pipe down and picked up the candle and the box of matches. There were two matches left in the box.

I removed one and stroked the head against the rough strip of paper on the side of the box. A bright flame rose like a small orange flower from the end of the stick. I held it to the wick of the candle and let the melting wax drip down on the table next to the pile of papers. There were remnants of wax already on the table and each of the new drips conjoined effortlessly to build a small semi fluid mound. I waited until the mass turned from clear to opaque, before turning over the candle to press it down in the center of the mound.

The melted wax rose like miniature waves around the base.

I held the candle in place until I was certain the wax had cooled.

I let go of the candle and picked up the bowl of gruel. It was warm and the smell of oats and pork fat rose from its content. Although it was difficult to determine the other ingredients, the taste wasn't entirely unpleasant and I slowly chewed at the salty mushy lumps until the bowl was empty.

I put the bowl back on the tray, picked up the battered metal cup and lifted it to my lips. The crystal clear water was cold and delicious. I swallowed a couple of mouthfuls before carefully replacing the cup.

I rubbed my hands together and was about to pick up the pipe, when I heard a murmurous noise coming from the window. It sounded like the rustle of leaves in the wind.

I stood up, walked over to the window and peeked out through the glassless opening. A raven was sitting on the windowsill outside.

Its head was slightly turned and an obsidian eye was staring at me from the other side of the mesh.

The raven's gaze was remarkably hypnotic and I had the impression that I was looking into a tiny bottomless well.

The raven broke the spell by ruffling its back feathers and shaking its tail.

"Good Evening Enoch Soule." It said. "How are you doing?" Its voice was placid and mellifluent.

I was startled by the bird's unexpected action and automatically took a step back. The raven didn't seem at all surprised by my behaviour.

Rather it kept looking at me while I attempted to collect myself.

"You can talk?" I said, when I had finally composed myself.

"You are very observant," the raven replied.

"How do you know my name?" I asked.

"You told me."

"Are you sure? I don't recall us meeting." I moved closer to the window.

"Yes, I am sure," the raven said. "In fact you have told me your name for as long as I can remember."

"What is that supposed to mean?" I asked.

"Exactly what I just said. You have told me your name for as long as I can remember."

"When did we first meet?" I asked, looking at the bird, which was busy cleaning a feather on its left wing.

"We have always met like this," the raven replied.

It looked at me with the inky eye.

"That makes no sense," I said. "That makes no sense at all. That would indicate that there's no before or after your arrival here. However, you just arrived, so you must have been somewhere else before you came."

"I have always been here, as have you.," the raven said. "There is no before or after. We are always here."

"Listen," I said, shaking my head, "when I looked out the window earlier this evening, I didn't see you. Ergo, you must have been somewhere else."

"Just because you didn't see me, doesn't mean I wasn't there. I was there, but you didn't see me. Now you see me and I am here."

"That's nonsensical," I said. "Your statement is absurd. The simple truth is: I would have seen you, if you were there. However, you weren't there, so I didn't see you." I paused and looked through the mesh. "Unless you can make yourself invisible that is."

"Don't be ridiculous," the raven said. "Of course I can't make myself invisible, that would be fantastical.

I am as real as anything I have told you." It jumped on the windowsill and looked at me.

I looked into the raven's left eye. It was a radiant icy blue.

In the darkness it seemed singularly alive, as if something phosphorous emanated from within. I gazed into the brightness, until the bird turned its head and the fulgid light dissipated.

I ignored the raven's last statement.

"Do you know what I am doing here?" I asked instead.

"This is what you are doing here," the raven answered without mordancy.

"Besides this," I said, "do you have any idea why I am here?"

"You are here for the same reason I am here."

"Could you then please tell me what you are doing here?" I asked.

"I thought you might be able to tell me that, "the raven answered paradoxically.

I ran my fingers through my hair and scratched at my beard.

It was evident that I wasn't gaining much information about my incarceration from my feathered visitor. Instead I ran my finger over one of the scribbles on the wall next to the window.

the stars look very different today

"Do you know who created all this?" I asked, gesturing behind me.

"You did," said the raven.

"That's not possible. It was all here when I arrived. I couldn't possibly have made all this in the short time I've been here."

"You are here and it is here."

"That's just another ambiguous statement. It doesn't make any sense."

"It makes perfect sense," the raven said. "Everything is here."

Although I could feel myself getting frustrated by the inanity of the bird's

153

statements, I refused to enter into an argument about the improbability of it all. Instead I inhaled deeply and surveyed the bird while it cleaned its feathers. Each time it dragged a feather through its beak and released it, there was a gentle swishing sound, that reminded me of the ebb and flow of the sea.

I looked into the horizon, but saw nothing but the dense fog.

"When did I arrive?" I asked after a while.

"For as long as I can remember, you have always been here."

The raven looked at me with its inky eye.

"That's preposterous," I said, promptly forgetting not to get myself worked up by the bird's answers. "Look around. It must have taken a considerable amount of time for one person to construct this."

"Time is never waiting," the raven said. "It's script-less and senseless. It's never hanging around for anyone to catch up. You are dancing an eternal waltz to the sound of your own beating heart. When the music stops, time has already moved on."

"I don't understand," I said, not mentioning the blatant triviality of the bird's last declaration. "Are you saying that I am trapped in this cell like a prisoner and that I have made all of these?" I gestured with my hands to the walls around me.

"Is that of importance?" the raven asked, with its head cocked.

"Of course it is. It's as important as the difference between being locked in

this cell and freedom."

"I see," it said, and flapped its wings. The sound vibrated in the stillness of the night.

"What do you see? I asked with exasperation. "What exactly do you see?"

"Everything that is here," the raven replied.

"Where are we exactly?"

"We are here," the bird replied genially.

I walked back to the table and sat down on the stool.

I picked up the pipe and stuck the black tip between my teeth and reached for the box of matches.

 I removed the last match, held it between my thumb and forefinger and stroked it against the side of the box. A small brilliant flame shot out from the end of the stick. I carefully placed it over the pipe and looked at the flame gamboling through the tobacco strands. When the pipe was well lit, I blew out the flame and placed the match on the table next to the candle.

The billowing smoke hovered above me like a hazy sea.

I looked up at the languid undulations, before I stood up and walked back to the window, where the raven was looking at me searchingly.

"We are here, until we are not," it said. "Before now, there was nothing, and after now there will be nothing. All there is is here."

It turned its head to one side then the other, looking at me expectantly.

"Then why are you here?" I asked.

"I am here because you are here."

"We are going round in circles," I said. "I am not any closer to finding out what I am doing here." I shook my head, then I looked up. "Although, if you are here because I am here, we must surely have met before." I looked at the raven. "Why can't I remember?"

"Look in the mirror," it said. "Perhaps you will find the answer to your question."

"What mirror?" I looked closely around the room.

The raven motioned with its head to the window pane next to me.

It was dark and I could see very little, so I walked over to the table, laid the pipe on the tabletop and put my hand around the candle. It made a muted popping sound when I gently pried it off the table.

I held my hand protectively around the flame, as I slowly walked back to look at my reflection in the glass.

I almost let go off the candle and had to steady it with a shaky hand.

An aged version of myself was looking back at me.

I leant towards the glass to examine my reflection.

My beard was peppered with silver specks and my longish wavy hair was almost white. A deep swell of furrows were running over my forehead and the lines around my eyes were spreading their leafless crowns across my temples, like sharply defined miniature trees. My grey violaceous lips looked shrunken and my skin was ashen and withered like a piece of discoloured parchment.

The most astonishing transformation was the colour of my eyes. The right eye was as black as the bottom of a well and the left was the colour of an iceberg.

I gazed at them silently, utterly perplexed by the transfigurement.

"When did this happen?" I asked, after I had regained my composure.

"What do you mean?" the raven said, looking at me intently with its dark eye.

"When did I get to be like this?" I asked, pointing at my face.

"You have always been like that," the raven said.

"That cannot possibly be true," I retorted. "I can't have been like this forever. I have aged and my eyes have different colours. In fact they are exactly the same colour as yours."

"You have always been like that," the raven said again, jumping from one side of the sill to the other.

"Even if that is the case, don't you find it extraordinary that we have the same colour eyes?" I asked.

"We have the same colour eyes because we are the same."

"That's yet another of your bizarre statements," I said, irritated.

"Don't you see that's completely illogical?" I shook my head and walked back to the table to replace the candle.

I dripped a bit of wax in the already established hollow and pushed the base of the candle into the molten mass.

I was standing by the table, when I heard a sharp sound behind me. The raven was now sitting on the other side of the glass, repeatedly tapping on the pane with its beak.

I turned around and walked back to the window.

Though it was dark, I could see the raven was moving its head back and forth, looking at me studiously.

"What do you see?" it asked.

"I see you."

"What am I?"

"You're a raven."

"Now look at you." It beckoned.

I searched for my own reflection in the glass.

"What do you see?"

The raven gazed at me with its obsidian eye.

Aside from myself, I believed I saw a hazy prismatic spiral move far beneath the shiny blank surface.

"A raven." I replied.

I awoke standing by the window in the watch room, looking into the darkness of my right eye that was reflected in the small mirror I was holding in my hand.

I was dressed in my long underwear, undershirt and a pair of woolen socks. It was late in the afternoon and quite cool in the room. Outside it was hard to disassociate the sea from the sky. Only the tiny dark strip in the horizon separated the leaden surfaces from one another.

I looked behind me.

On the table stood a solitary white candle.

The light from the flickering flame flowed like a slow moving rivulet over the exterior of a small pile of paper lying on the table next to it. I walked over to the table and picked up the papers and flicked through them. Every single page was empty. I put the pile back down on the table.

They spread out like a monochrome fan on the table top.

I am at a loss to the meaning of any of this. I don't know, if what I saw in the glass was merely a dream or by some means a premonition. I believe a great amount of matter is swirling around me and that I am somehow trapped in the center, like an involuntary accomplice in a complex schedule of inexplicable events.

It disturbs me that I couldn't recall much in the cell and that the things I could remember seemed impalpable.

Although it is difficult for me to understand what is happening in my dream state, I am convinced that I have always been and will always be of sound mind and that my somnambular disposition is nothing but a minor inconvenience.

He turned over the last piece of paper to see if there was anything written on the back, before he put it down on the pile on the left.

The back of the sheet was blank.

He removed his fingerless gloves, rubbed his hands together and stared at the space in front of him. He wondered if the story he just read was the last or whether Soule had continued to write down his dreams, but for one reason or another, hadn't included them in the pile.

He unraveled the scarf from the teapot, wrapped it around his neck and put on his gloves.

The chair made a loud scraping sound on the floor, as he got up and walked over to the window.

The light had changed dramatically.

The sun had begun its ascent and its proliferating rays were spreading out like a dynamic fiery blanket on the surface of the ocean.

He had been gazing into the distance for quite some time, when he noticed a tiny movement in the horizon.

It was like a small black particle of dust suspended in the air.

He didn't quite know what to make of it and half expected it to disappear, but it grew in size and he finally realized that it was a bird flying towards the tower.

He shaded his eyes with his hand and looked at the advancing bird.

The morning sun made it difficult for him to see, so he crossed the room to retrieve the binoculars. He then walked back to the window to search the horizon.

He located the bird almost immediately.

It was slowly closing in.

He observed it through the binoculars. He didn't recognize the flight pattern. The movements of the wings were too brisk to be a seagull and the bird didn't glide at all, which ruled out any of the seafaring birds with which he was familiar.

He abruptly lowered the binoculars.

A cold sweat appeared on his forehead and he suddenly felt nauseated. He removed his gloves and pulled at his scarf to let in the cold morning air.

Above the sound of the sea below, his shallow breath sounded wheezy and exaggerated in the otherwise quiet room. His palms were sweating and his hands shaking as he again lifted the binoculars.

The bird had made considerable progress; what he saw only confirmed what his instinct had already told him.

"You," he said.

He let the binoculars drop. They hung heavily around his neck, resting on his chest like a dead weight, as he stared at the approaching bird.

It was close now.

He thought he could hear the sound of wings pushing against the air as the bird neared the tower, although that was absurd.

The raven landed on the windowsill and looked at him through the glass. It turned it head to one side then the other and his suspicion was affirmed.

The right eye was dark as ebony and the left like a brilliant gem lying on a piece of black velvet.

The raven stared at him through the glass.

When it finally spoke, it was as if the sound emanated from all around.

"Do you know who you are?" it said.

For a moment he just stared at the bird, then he threw back his head and laughed.

He laughed until his patulous laughter lay siege to the room.

He stopped laughing and looked at the raven.

"I know who I am," he said.

"I know who I am."

Dear S,

I hope that this letter finds you well and that you have settled into your new position in a satisfactory manner.

I understand that you are most likely engrossed in work, so you will have to forgive me if you find this letter and the dreams of ES to be an encumbrance. However, I have a strong desire to share these tales with someone who, perhaps better than anybody, understands the instability of the human mind.

I hope you recalled the conversation we had, when we met in B and I encouraged you to read the dreams before you read this letter. I do hope that you followed my advice, so as to enter into the narrative of ES with an open and immaculate mind.

As you know, the subject of ES has given me great concern and weighed heavily upon my shoulders during these past two decades. You are of course aware that I share with you the belief that there is a point of some importance to the ease and comfort of the person, who is so unhappy as to be deprived of their normal reason, and that we must see to it that adequate provision is offered to those who cannot help themselves.

I have, as you also practice, endeavoured to provide a place of confinement, where the unlucky soul can be attended by physicians who believe that the miserable can someday have their reasoning restored.

However, before I give you a brief account of the life of ES before he came into my care, it saddens me to say that he is no longer a patient of mine. By some extraordinary coincidence, he passed away only the day after I posted the package containing his writings and this letter to you.

An orderly passing his cell heard him laugh rather loudly and persistently. When he suddenly stopped, the orderly slid aside the door hatch to check on the patient. He raised the alarm, when he saw the patient on the floor in the cell. When I finally arrived on the scene, it was unfortunately too late. ES was lying on the floor with his arms spread away from his body. His mouth looked like it was formed around a word and his eyes were blankly gazing at the ceiling.

Two weeks yesterday, I had him interred within the institutional grounds. Besides the priest, my wife and I were the only people present. It was a short but emotional ceremony and I thanked the priest profusely for his thoughtful and enlightened eulogy. Befitting the occasion, the lowly cemetery was blanketed in a thick fog, that made us all appear as if we were instruments in one of ES's peculiar narratives. I had asked our carpenter to make a small wooden cross upon which he, per my behest, had inscribed the words 'The stars look very different today' on the crossbeam.

I expect you might find it to be a rather sentimental gesture from a professional physician to allow such a personal pennant, and you would normally be correct, but I believe ES deserved something from his own remarkable fantasies to accompany him in the hereafter, whatever that might be. He died alone and although I realize that that statement will be countered by the rationalist with the fact that we all do, I do however find his exceptional tale most tragic and hope that my supplicatory benefaction will somehow find its way to him.

I remember not giving you much information about ES and his particular condition when we last met, so for your information I have included a short and rather incomplete description so that you might have a better perception of his affliction.

ES was brought to my institution some twenty years back (the exact date and time is unfortunately not recorded). He had been found in B, sleeping on a pier in the harbor in early November. The night before, he had been observed by a first mate on a ship.

Apparently ES had been standing on the pier the entire night looking out over the sea. When the first mate had seen him lying on the pier in the morning, he had gone to see if he was still alive, as the weather was abnormally cold for that time of year. When he discovered that ES, who was barely breathing, was dressed in a lighthouse keeper's uniform, the first mate had fetched the harbor police, who in turn called upon the coast guard, who eventually brought ES into our care. At the time it was not known how long ES had been in B, but by piecing together the scant information I subsequently received, my educated guess would be that he had been in B for about six to eight months. He was in a most terrible physical state. He was awfully emaciated, his matted hair was filthy and his dirtied fingernails looked like the claws of an animal. He was apathetic and non-communicative, but accepted our help and allowed an orderly to undress and bathe him without incident. Besides the tattered uniform and a dirty woolen scarf he wore wrapped around his neck, we found only the cover of a small book in his possession. All of the pages had been torn out and although I might have speculated to their content many a time, it is however impossible to say what they may have contained. I was not yet the physician in charge of him and although the patient's progress was often discussed amongst the staff, there were many other souls that required my assistance and I did not see him for quite a considerable amount of time. Roughly a year must have gone by, before we were finally introduced.

Before I enter into a professional explanation of the patient's symptoms and general conduct, I would like to inform you of the known details that seemed to have caused the breakdown in his reasoning and in his ensuing behaviour. As far as I am aware there are two major factors associated with his rapid declension. Firstly the horrific and unexpected death of his wife and his two daughters and secondly his long and lonely imprisonment in the confines of the lighthouse. We know that the two separate events coincided, however we are not aware of how he came to know about his family's tragic demise.

What is known is this: It appears that ES' s wife and daughters had planned a surprise visit to P and that they had secretly purchased tickets on the ill-fated steamship leaving B destined for P. As you are well aware of the terrible fate of that ship, I shall spare you the details. Suffice it is to say that a considerable number of lives were lost in that historic gale. However, it has been impossible to verify the deaths of ES's wife and daughters, as the only known passenger list went down with the ship. We can only assume by their continued absence, that they did indeed succumb to the waves that night, and that ES, by some inexplicable means, was informed of their demise. The gale that wrecked such havoc on the Eastern shore and killed countless people, also effectively trapped ES in his tower. From my conversations with his employer, the U.S. Coast Guard, he was alone in the lighthouse for at least fifty three days, perhaps even longer. After the disastrous effects of the gale, most people had been concerned with repairing the extensive damage caused and no one had thought to bring him new provisions, and although his supplies were running low at the end, he had enough kerosene left to heat the stove in the galley and to light the lens. To our knowledge he continued to perform his duties and subsisted on a diet of oats, beans, dried pork, tea and sugar, which was all that was left in the pantry, before help finally arrived.

It was but a stroke of luck that it was discovered he was missing. The Coast Guard had assigned a new keeper to the lighthouse to relieve ES, and it was he who immediately informed the Coast Guard that ES was missing from his post. It was first assumed that something unexpected had happened. However, the new keeper could not find any evidence of an accident and although none of ES's personal belongings could be found in or around the lighthouse, he had nevertheless left everything else as if he was ready to return at any moment. The kettle was on the stove, the teapot had fresh leaves in it and a small white porcelain cup was half filled with water. This had so confounded the new lighthouse keeper, that he mentioned it to his employer, who in turn revealed it to me.

It is difficult to determine exactly when or how ES left the tower, but according to the accounts from the passing ships, the lighthouse had been operating every night, leading up to the very day of his disappearance. It is still a mystery how he managed to leave, what he did or where he lived in the months between leaving the lighthouse and when he was found sleeping on the pier in B habour.

As far as we know, ES has no surviving family members. His parents and an older unmarried brother are dead, as are, we assume, his wife and his two daughters. His wife Emily was an only child and her parents died in the fire in 1872, when she was still a young girl. She was raised by an aunt in N before marrying ES. When ES's estate was sold, the Coast Guard attempted to contact the aunt, but she had moved away from the area with no forwarding address, so in the end the Coast Guard elected to provide our institution with the necessary cash reserve to keep E.S. as a patient for as long as we deemed it necessary. The money was sufficient to keep E.S. comfortable for the rest of his natural life and his former employer stopped querying about his progress more than a decade ago, most likely because our answers never varied.

When ES became a patient at the institution, he was initially placed in the common area. However, an array of factors made it difficult for us to keep him with the other patients. Due to his deeply ingrained personal habits, his daily routine and internal system was directly opposite to the other patients. He would sleep for most of the day and although his somnambulistic behaviour was manageable and his general demeanor non aggressive, his nightly escapades nevertheless had a profoundly upsetting effect on a large number his fellow patients. As you know, we do our best not to restrain our patients unless absolutely necessary, but though we attempted to alter his behaviour, the nightly wanderings unfortunately created a variety of commotions that were extremely difficult for us to ease. A large number of our exceedingly frail patients became so agitated by his actions, that they had to be restrained at night.

We endeavoured to change his behaviour, but after a few months, and after a particularly long night spent calming down other patients, it was decided that ES was to be moved to one of the cells, that were normally used for our most troubled patients. That is where I, as his assigned physician, met him for the first time.

When I first met him on his own, he was standing by the window looking outside, but was otherwise unresponsive. Although it did seem like his eyes were following the movements of the birds in the sky, he didn't turn around when I entered the room or when I addressed him by name. In fact there were no response to any external stimuli and there was no obvious sign of a startle reflex. I lead him by the arm to the stool where he sat down. He passively permitted me to listen to his breathing and to his heart. His physical condition was, all things considered, good, and I could find nothing wrong with his motor skills, nor with his physical reflexes. I explained to him why I was there and talked to him about the tests I was performing. I attempted, as is usual when treating a patient, to behave as if this was an altogether normal interaction. The entire time I was there, he gazed unseeingly into the distance. Not once did he acknowledge that he was sharing his cell with another human being. However, my initial belief that ES was completely passive was wrong. You see, he was capable of quite a few specific tasks. For instance, he could move voluntarily and he didn't need help with feeding. The orderly would push the food tray through the hatch and at some point during the day or night the food would disappear. When I visited there was often an empty tray standing on the table, and yet I never saw him consume anything. Also, after being placed in the cell he never once soiled himself. At night, during his continued nightly excursions, he would, again unobserved, use the bucket provided.

He spent his day standing by the window or sitting by the table in the cell, as if he was a performer in a silent play. To my knowledge he never spoke a word during these sessions and none of the night guards or orderlies that I interviewed, ever heard him say anything at all.

On my early encounters with ES in the general ward, I was convinced that he was suffering from a combination of narcolepsy and stupor brought on by a traumatic event. I believed then that he was exhibiting all the standard symptoms of those particular afflictions. However, after visiting him in his cell and observing his progress, I later began to hypothesize that ES had originally entered into a deep depressive state due to the tragic death of his family and that he at some point afterwards suffered from an inflammation of the brain, possibly Encephalitis Lethargica, causing the disturbance in his sleep pattern and the ensuing catatonic state. Although I realize not all of the resulting symptoms fit that theory, it would certainly explain the extensive behavioral changes and the hallucinatory narrative in his stories.

In the first couple of years, I visited ES three to four times a week. In that time there was no noticeable change in his behaviour. During the day he was asleep and in the evenings, when I would normally visit, he was in the same passive state as when I first met him. I one day discussed my patient's lack of progress with Dr. K, with whom you are familiar, and it was under his supervision, that we attempted electroshock therapy to see if we could somehow restore or at least alter the patient's behavioral pattern. Alas, the experiment was less than successful as ES seemed to retreat even further into his self-created adytum. He also temporarily lost control of both his motor skills and his bodily functions as a result, so we halted the therapy after eight sessions and never repeated them.

After a couple of months ES seemed to settle back into his old routine. He was not self- harming or aggressive and in no way a danger to himself or others, so I decided to revert to my former strategy and only use verbal communication in my dealings with him.

Years went by with no radical change in his general attitude and ES continued to function as well as could be expected. However, it was one day discovered that he had begun writing on the walls in the cell. It took some time for me to realize this, due to the fact that the walls in the cell were already covered with small inscriptions made by previous patients and that his initial scribbles were close to the ground by the bed. An orderly who was in charge of changing the bed linen discovered that ES had used a small piece of grit to scrape his initials on the wall next to the name of his wife.

I was immediately convinced that this was a breakthrough and believed that I had finally managed, through my countless monologues, to rouse something vital within him that had eventually come bubbling to the surface. After the writings were discovered I had an intensive session with ES where I talked specifically about the constitutive memories he might still have of his wife and daughters. He was entirely passive throughout the session and seemed as remote as ever. On the ensuing session, I began to monitor his writings and to copy them in my journal. I had hoped that he would utilize the writings as a direct communication and that he would somehow show me that he understood what had happened to him or where he was. Unfortunately that was not the case. The first sentence was proof that ES believed himself to be someplace else entirely. 'The sea is calm', he wrote on the wall by the window. It was clear to me then, that he believed himself to be in the lighthouse still.

Although it was highly inadvisable to supply a patient with an instrument with which he could harm himself, I nonetheless had the carpenter fashion a small wooden handle on which he inserted a small dull piece of metal, that could be used as a rudimentary writing tool. Following my next session with ES, I left the tool behind on the table and ordered an orderly to keep watch, in case ES attempted to harm himself. I had no reason to worry.

The next time I visited his cell, I realized why.

On the wall above his bed ES had started to write the letter to his wife that you have already read at the beginning of his tale. He was more than halfway through and I again tried to talk to him about his actions, but he was completely unresponsive and didn't in any way demonstrate whether he knew I was talking to him.

Throughout the next year, ES continued to fill the walls in his cell with words and sometimes drawings. On each of my regular visits, I made sure to write down everything he wrote or drew. I then began to pin up the notes in my office, to see if I could discover any specific connecting elements that could aid in the healing of his mind. I must admit it took me a while to understand that there was a definitive system to his writing. Rather than the despaired ravings of a lost soul, ES was through his script describing a complex and multilayered story, that although bizarre, I found exceptionally fascinating.

Soon after I discovered that there was an aspect of lucidity in his writings, I gave a detailed account of the patient's case, and the extraordinary development surrounding it, to a selective group of my fellow physicians. Everyone seemed astounded by this intriguing development and after consulting with Dr. K., it was agreed to supply E.S. with the appropriate writing tools and a daily quantity of paper to encourage him on his way to recovery. I introduced the items immediately and although ES's general behaviour and his attitude towards me remained unchanged, he began, almost instantly, to write down the story you have just read. As he only wrote at night during his somnambulations, we supplied him with a candle so he could see what he was writing in the dark. When I later realized that he was an enthusiastic smoker, I added the pipe and the tobacco, initially to ease his anguish, but mainly so he could feel more human. Although he had no trouble lightning the pipe or smoking the tobacco, there was never any indication that he understood why or how the pipe and tobacco appeared. They were quite simply accepted as the other basic elements in his confined life. When he finished the tobacco, he just replaced the pipe on the tray. I never even knew if he enjoyed the tobacco I bought.

I am currently in possession of at least twelve different manuscripts, all telling a slightly different variation of the same story. Each manuscript essentially has the same structure and narrative, but each also has its own unique departure from the norm. For instance, in some of the stories the bull is black not white, and sometimes the black raven is white and vice versa. Also, it seems that the eyes of the raven change colour from time to time. Most peculiarly though, some of the characters seem to alternate.

As an example: In one of the stories, the poet Poe is to be found in the well, *where he has a conversation with the white raven about poetry.*

The man Toru is, in the same story, found to be inhabiting Poe's body in the cemetery, where he talks to the black raven about a lost cat. There are probably a slew of other permutations that I have overlooked, but these are, as far as I am aware, some of the more significant changes. I will be more than happy to share these manuscripts with you, should you wish to read them as well. However, the most significant alteration is the addition of the last chapter. It is the only time ES ever wrote about or described his immediate situation. I found the manuscript on the table in his cell the day he passed away.

I have of course speculated at length about the meaning of the dreams and the overall narrative of ES and while I believe it has been possible to make sense of some of the more rational accounts, through my own analysis and the conversations I have had with my fellow physicians on the subject, I must admit I have found many of the tales especially difficult to decipher. I know you are an ardent follower of the latest development of the use of dreams in therapy. I would therefore very much appreciate your professional insight.

I am especially interested in reading your interpretation of the fact that ES, in his apparently 'lucid' state, wrote as an observer about his own experience as a lighthouse keeper, and that he as such, read his own writing not realizing that the words belonged to him. Also, I am intrigued to know, if you differentiate between the dreams that have a base in reality and the dreams that are merely fantastical.

I wish that I had thought to ask for your help earlier, but as you have been busy building your own successful career, I always feared it would be too much of an imposition. I am however very much looking forward to reading your professional diagnosis and wait for your answer with anticipation. I truly appreciate your help in this matter. If truth be told, the case of ES has cast a significant shadow upon my life for so long and I hope that your diagnosis will provide just a modicum of much needed clarity to the meaning of it all.

Yours sincerely,

E

He flicked the last sheet of paper down on the expansive tabletop. It floated like a thin membrane on the smooth lacquered surface and came to rest next to the small heap of papers lying near the edge.

He gazed into the distance as he listened to the raindrops beating on the windowpane. He put his hands on the table, pushing the chair away behind him as he stood up.

He slowly walked to the window.

He pulled his jacket close around his neck and looked into the darkness outside.

What had started as a slight drizzle in the early evening, had turned into a veritable downpour that now completely obscured his view.

He poured himself a drink.

The amber liquid flowed like a miniature waterfall from the decanter, and splashed into the bottom of the heavy crystal glass.

He lifted the glass to his lips. He appreciated the almost conflagrant sensation on his tongue. He swirled the liquid around in his mouth before he swallowed.

He waited for the warmth to suffuse his body, as he picked up the pipe and the red can of tobacco from the low blackwood coffee table. He pushed the tobacco into the bowl of a dark briar pipe and lit it with a match that he removed from a small box in his jacket pocket.

There were two matches left.

As he inhaled and exhaled, he looked at the undulating flame weaving its way in and out of the tobacco strands. He blew the smoke into the air, replaced the can on the coffee table and looked at the thin hazy blanket undulating in the air high above his head.

He walked back to the window and tapped on the glass with the end of the pipe.

For a while nothing happened.

He tapped on the windowpane once more and then he at last heard the sound of wings pushing against the air.

The sound stopped and he looked through the glass.

Outside two ravens were sitting on the windowsill.

One was iridescent black and the other ivory white.

They were quietly watching him.

He looked at his reflection in the windowpane.

His eyes were staring back at him. The right was as dark as the bottom of a well and the other icy blue and brilliant as a sapphire. "Why have you called on us keeper of the lighthouse?" The ravens asked in unison.

The sound appeared as if it was spoken from a place inside his head.

"We have work to do," he answered.

As he opened the window to let in the birds, a delicate membrane of wet cold formed on his skin.

"We are here." They sang in concert, flying through the air.

"We are here."

He picked up the manuscript from the table, walked over to the fireplace and tossed it in the fire.

The near diaphanous sheets submitted to the fiery embrace like a long lost lover.

From the back of the chair the devouring flames were reflected in the eyes of the ravens.

He sat back down in the chair and gazed at the piece of paper lying on the table in front of him.

The sheet was small, not much bigger than a regular postcard, and almost translucent. It was blank.

He picked up the quill and dipped the tip in the inkwell.

In the background he could hear the sound of waves crashing against the rocks.

Acknowledgements

I would like to thank my editor and friend Kavi Montanaro for his guidance, insightful advice and patience in the writing of this book. Without the countless conversations and his unwavering enthusiasm for the plight of Enoch Soule, one can only speculate how this manuscript would have presented itself.

Thanks also to Christian O'Connor for his shrewd and humorous caffeine induced input.

I am forever indebted to Kyle Louis Fletcher for lending his time and his marvelously creative talent to the cover design and artwork of this book.

Thanks also to Rita Stringfellow for her continued support during this undertaking.

I would also like to give my sincere thanks to Jesper Magnusson for his ardent belief in me. His changeless loyalty over the years has been next to none and is very much appreciated.

Finally I would like to thank my wife Helen for her endless optimism, her never failing words of reassurance and her invaluable support throughout the entire process.

This manuscript is set in Iowan Old Style. It was designed in 1990 by John Downer, a renowned sign painter. Iowan Old Style is a hardy, contemporary text design modeled after earlier revivals of Jenson and Griffo typefaces but with a larger x-height, tighter letterfit and proportioned capitals.

 ANGRY OWL